illustrated by Harry Bishop

Illustrated Classics

THE ADVENTURES OF TOM SAWYER

Mark Twain

Derrydale Books

New York

Aunt Polly

"Tom!"

No answer.

"Tom!"

No answer.

"What's gone with that boy, I wonder? You, Tom!"

The old lady pulled her spectacles down and looked over them, about the room; then she put them up and looked out.

"Well, I lay if I get hold of you, I'll—"

She did not finish, for by this time she was bending down and punching under the bed with the broom—and so she needed breath to punctuate the punches with. She resurrected nothing but the cat.

"I never did see the beat of that boy!"

She went to the open door and stood in it, and looked out among the tomato vines and 'jimpson' weeds that constituted the garden. No Tom. So she lifted up her voice, at an angle calculated for distance, and shouted:

"Y-o-u-u Tom!"

There was a slight noise behind her, and she turned just in time to seize a small boy by the slack of his roundabout and arrest his flight. "There! I migh 'a thought of that closet. What you been doing in there?"

"Nothing."

"Nothing! Look at your hands, and look at your mouth. What is that truck?"

"I don't know, Aunt."

"Well, I know. It's jam, that's what it is. Forty times I've said if you didn't let that jam alone I'd skin you. Hand me that switch."

The switch hovered in the air. The peril was desperate.

"My! Look behind you, Aunt!"

The old lady whirled around and snatched her skirts out of danger, and the lad fled, on the instant, scrambled up the high board fence, and disappeared over it. His Aunt Polly stood surprised a moment, and then broke into a gentle laugh.

"Hang the boy, can't I ever learn anything? Ain't he played me tricks enough, but, he's my own dead sister's boy, poor thing, and I ain't got the heart to lash him somehow. Every time I let him off my conscience does hurt me so; and every time I hit him my old heart 'most breaks. Well-a-well, man that is born of woman is of few days and full of trouble, as the Scripture says, and I reckon it's so. He'll play hookey this evening, and I'll just be obliged to make him work tomorrow, to punish him. It's mighty hard to make him work Saturdays, when all the boys is having a holiday, but he hates work more than he hates anything else, and I've got to do some of my duty by him, or I'll be the ruination of the child."

The Fight

Tom did play hookey, and he had a very good time. He got back home barely in season to help Jim, the small coloured boy, saw next day's wood, and split the kindlings before supper.

The summer evenings were long. It was not dark yet. Presently Tom checked his stride. A stranger was before him; a boy a shade larger than himself. A new-comer of any age or either sex was an impressive curiosity in the poor little village of St. Petersburg. This boy was well dressed, too well dressed on a week-day. The more Tom stared at the splendid marvel, the higher he turned up his nose at his finery, and the shabbier and shabbier his own outfit seemed to him to grow. Neither boy spoke. If one moved the other moved—but only sidewise, in a circle. They kept face to face and eye to eye all the time. Finally, Tom said:

"I can lick you!"

"I'd like to see you try it."

"Well, I can do it."

"No you can't, either."

"Yes I can."

"No you can't."

"I can."

"You can't."

"Can."

"Can't."

Tom drew a line in the dust with his big toe, and said:

"I dare you to step over that, and I'll lick you till you can't stand up. Anybody that'll take a dare will steal a sheep."

The new boy stepped over promptly, and said:

"Now you said you'd do it, now let's see you do it then."

"Don't you crowd me, now; you'd better look out, or else."

"Well, you said you'd do it—why don't you do it? Bet you can't."

"By jingoes, for two cents I will do it."

The new boy took two broad coppers out of his pocket and held them out with derision.

Tom struck them to the ground.

In an instant both boys were rolling and tumbling in the dirt, gripped together like cats; and for the space of a minute they tugged and tore at each other's hair and clothes, punched and scratched each other's noses, and covered themselves with dust and glory. Presently the confusion took form, and through the fog of battle Tom appeared, seated astride the new boy, and pounding him with his fists.

"Hollar 'nuff!" said he.

The boy only struggled to free himself. He was crying, mainly from rage.

"Hollar 'nuff!" and the pounding went on.

At last the stranger got out a smothered "nuff!" and Tom let him up, and said, "Now that'll learn you. Better look out who you're fooling with next time."

He got home pretty late that night, and when he climbed cautiously in at the window he uncovered an ambuscade in the person of his aunt; and when she saw the state his clothes were in, her resolution to turn his Saturday holiday into captivity at hard labour became adamantine in its firmness.

Tom's Punishment

Saturday morning was come, and all the summer world was bright and fresh, and brimming with life.

Tom appeared on the side-walk with a bucket of white-wash and a long-handled brush. He surveyed the fence, and the gladness went out of nature, and a deep melancholy settled down upon his spirit. Thirty yards of broad fence nine feet high! It seemed to him that life was hollow, and existence but a burden. Sighing, he dipped his brush and passed it along the topmost plank; repeated the operation; did it again; compared the insignificant whitewashed streak with the far-reaching continent of un-whitewashed fence, and sat down on a tree-box discouraged. Jim came skipping out at the gate with a tin pail, and singing Buffalo Gals. Bringing water from the town pump had always been hateful work in Tom's eyes before, but now it did not strike him so.

"Say, Jim; I'll fetch the water if you'll whitewash some."

Jim shook his head, and said:

"Can't, Mar's Tom. Ole missis she tole me I got to go an' git dis water an' not stop foolin' 'roun' wid anybody."

"Oh, never you mind what she said, Jim. That's the way she always talks. Gimme the bucket—I won't be gone only a minute. She won't ever know."

"Oh, I dasn't, Mar's Tom. Ole missis she'd take an' tar de head off'n me. 'Deed she would."

"Jim, I'll give you a marble. I'll give you a white alley!"

Jim began to waver.

"White alley, Jim; and it's a bully tow."

"My; dat's a mighty gay marvel, I tell you. But, Mar's Tom, I's powerful 'fraid ole missis."

But Jim was only human—this attention was too much for him. He put down his pail, took the white alley. In another minute he was flying down the street with his pail and a tingling rear, Tom was whitewashing with vigour, and Aunt Polly was retiring from the field with a slipper in her hand and triumph in her eye.

But Tom's energy did not last. He began to think of the fun he had planned for this day, and his sorrows multiplied. At this dark and hopeless moment an inspiration burst upon him. Nothing less than a great, magnificent inspiration. He took up his brush and went tranquilly to work. Ben Rogers hove in sight presently; the very boy of all boys whose ridicule he had been dreading. Ben's gait was the hop, skip and jump—proof enough that his heart was light and his anticipations high. He was eating an apple, and giving a long melodious whoop at intervals, followed by a deep-toned ding dong dong, ding dong dong, for he was personating a steamboat! As he drew near he slackened speed, took the middle of the street, leaned far over to starboard, and rounded-to ponderously, and with laborious pomp and circumstance, for he was personating the Big Missouri, and considered himself to be drawing deep water. He was boat, and captain, and engine-bells combined, so he had to imagine himself standing on his own hurricane-deck giving the orders and executing them.

"Stop her, sir! Ling-a-ling-ling." The headway ran almost out, and he drew up slowly towards the side-walk. "Ship up to back! Ling-a-ling-ling!" His arms straightened and stiffened down his sides.

"Set her back on the starboard! Ling-a-ling-ling! Chow! ch-chow-wow-chow!" his right hand mean-time describing stately circles, for it was representing a forty-foot wheel. "Let her go back on the labboard! Ling-a-ling-ling! Chow-ch-chow-chow!" The left hand began to describe circles.

Tom went on whitewashing—paid no attention to the steamer. Ben stared a moment, and then said:

"Hi-yi! You're up a stump, ain't you!"

No answer. Tom surveyed his last touch with the eye of an artist; then he gave his brush another gentle sweep, and surveyed the result as before. Ben ranged up alongside of him. Tom's mouth watered for the apple, but he stuck to his work. Ben said:

"Hello, old chap; you got to work, hey?"

"Why, it's you, Ben! I warn't noticing."

"Say, I'm going in a swimming, I am. Don't you wish you could? But of course, you'd druther work, wouldn't you? 'Course you would!"

Tom contemplated the boy a bit, and said:

"What do you call work?"

"Why, ain't that work?"

Tom resumed his whitewashing, and answered carelessly:

"Well, maybe it is, and maybe it ain't. All I know is, it suits Tom Sawyer."

"Oh, come now, you don't mean you like it?"

The brush continued to move.

"Like it? Well, I don't see why I oughtn't to like it. Does a boy get a chance to whitewash a fence every day of his life?"

That put the thing in a new light. Ben stopped nibbling his apple. Tom swept his brush daintily back and forth—stepped back to note the effect—added a touch here and there—criticised the effect again, Ben watching every move, and getting more and more interested, more and more absorbed. Presently he said:

"Say, Tom, let me whitewash a little."

Tom considered; was about to consent; but he altered his mind: "No, no; I reckon it wouldn't hardly do, Ben. You see, Aunt Polly's awful particular about this fence—right here on the street, you know—but if it was the back fence I wouldn't mind, and she wouldn't. Yes, she's awful particular about this fence; it's got to be done very careful; I reckon there ain't one boy in a thousand, maybe two thousand, that can do it the way it's got to be done."

"No—is that so? Oh, come now; lemme just try, only just a little. I'd let you, if you was me, Tom."

"Ben, I'd like to, honest injun; but Aunt Polly—well, Jim wanted to do it, but she wouldn't let him. Sid wanted to do it, but she wouldn't let Sid. Now, don't you see how I am fixed? If you was to tackle this fence, and anything was to happen to it—"

"Oh, shucks; I'll be just as careful. Now lemme try. Say—I'll give you the core of my apple."

"Well, here. No, Ben; now don't; I'm afeard—"

"I'll give you all of it!"

Tom gave up the brush with reluctance in his face, but alacrity in his heart. And while the late steamer Big Missouri worked and sweated in the sun, the retired artist sat on a barrel in the shade close by, dangled his legs, munched his apple, and planned the slaughter of more innocents. There was no lack of material; boys happened along every little while; they came to jeer, but remained to whitewash. By the time Ben was fagged out, Tom had traded the next chance to Billy Fisher for a kite in good repair; and when he played out, Johnny Miller bought in for a dead rat and a string to swing it with; and so on, and so on, hour after hour. And when the middle of the afternoon came, from being a poor poverty-stricken boy in the morning, Tom was literally rolling in wealth. He had, besides the things I have mentioned, twelve marbles, part of a jew's harp, a piece of blue bottle-glass to look through, a spool-cannon, a key that wouldn't unlock anything, a fragment of chalk, a glass stopper of a decanter, a tin soldier, a couple of tadpoles, six fire-crackers, a kitten with only one eye, a brass door-knob, a dog

collar—but no dog—the handle of a knife, four pieces of orange-peel, and a dilapidated old window-sash. He had had a nice, good, idle time all the while—plenty of company—and the fence had three coats of whitewash on it! If he hadn't run out of whitewash he would have bankrupted every boy in the village.

Tom said to himself that it was not such a hollow world after all. He had discovered a great law of human action, without knowing it, namely, that, in order to make a man or a boy covet a thing, it is only necessary to make the thing difficult to attain.

Tom presented himself before Aunt Polly.

"Mayn't I go and play now, Aunt?"

"What, a'ready? How much have you done?"

"It's all done, Aunt."

"Tom, don't lie to me. I can't bear it."

"I ain't, Aunt; it is all done."

Aunt Polly placed small trust in such evidence. She went out to see for herself; and she would have

12

been content to find twenty per cent of Tom's statement true. When she found the entire fence whitewashed, and not only whitewashed but elaborately coated and recoated, and even a streak added to the ground, her astonishment was almost unspeakable. She said:

"Well, I never! There's no getting around it; you can work when you're a mind to, Tom." And then she diluted the compliment by adding, "But it's powerful seldom you're a mind to, I'm bound to say. Well, go 'long and play; but mind you get back some time in a week, or I'll tan you."

Tom's New Love

Tom was over the fence and gone. There was a gate, but as a general thing he was too crowded for time to make use of it.

As he was passing by the house where Jeff Thatcher lived, he saw a new girl in the garden—a lovely little blue-eyed creature with yellow hair plaited into two long tails, white summer frock, and embroidered pantalettes. The fresh-crowned hero fell without firing a shot. A certain Amy Lawrence vanished out of his heart, and left not even a memory of herself behind. He had thought he loved her to distraction; he had regarded his passion as adoration; and behold it was only a poor little evanescent partiality. He had been months winning her, she had confessed hardly a week ago; he had been the happiest and the proudest boy in the world only seven short days, and here, in one instant of time, she had gone out of his heart like a casual stranger whose visit is done.

He worshipped this new angel with furtive eye, till he saw that she had discovered him; then he pretended he did not know she was present, and began to "show off" in all sorts of absurd boyish ways in order to win her admiration. He kept up this grotesque foolishness for some little time; but by-and-by, while he was in the midst of some dangerous gymnastic performances, he glanced aside, and saw that the little girl was wending to the house. Tom came up to the fence, and leaned on it, grieving, and hoping she would tarry yet a while longer. She halted a moment on the steps, and then moved towards the door. Tom heaved a great sigh as she put her foot on the threshold, but his face lit up, right away, for she tossed a pansy over the fence a moment before she disappeared. The boy ran around and stopped within a short distance of the flower, and then shaded his eyes with his hand, and began to look down the street as if he had discovered something of interest going on in that direction. Presently he picked up a straw and began trying to balance it on his nose, with his head tilted far back; and as he moved from side to side in his efforts he edged nearer and nearer towards the pansy; finally his bare foot rested upon it, his pliant toes closed upon it, and he hopped away with his treasure, and disappeared around the corner. But only for a minute——only while he could button the flower inside his jacket, next his heart, or next his stomach possibly, for he was not much posted in anatomy and not hypercritical anyway.

He wandered far away from the accustomed haunts of boys, and sought desolate places that were in harmony with his spirit. A log raft in the river invited him, and he seated himself on its outer edge, and contemplated the dreary vastness of the stream, wishing the while that he could only be drowned all at once without going through the uncomfortable routine devised by nature. Then he thought of his flower. He got it out rumpled and wilted, and it increased his dismal felicity. He wondered if she would pity him if she knew! Would she cry, and wish that she had a right to put her arms around his neck and comfort him? Or would she turn coldly away like all the hollow world?

This picture brought such an agony of pleasurable

suffering that he worked it over and over again in his mind and set it up in varied lights till he wore it threadbare. At last he rose up sighing and departed in the darkness. About half past nine he came along the deserted street to where the adored unknown lived; he paused a moment, no sound fell upon his listening ear; a candle was casting a dull glow upon the curtain of a second-storey window. Was the sacred presence there? He climbed the fence, threaded his stealthy way through the plants, till he stood under that window; he looked up at it long, and with emotion; then he laid him down on the ground under it, disposing himself upon his back, with his hands clasped upon his breast, and holding his poor wilted flower. And thus he would die—out in the cold world with no shelter over his homeless head, no friendly hand to wipe the death-damps from his brow, no loving face to bend pityingly over him when the great agony came. And thus she would see him when she looked out upon the glad morning —and oh, would she drop one tear upon his lifeless form, would she heave one little sigh to see a bright young life so rudely blighted, so untimely cut down?

The window went up; a maid-servant's discordant voice broke the silence, and a deluge of water drenched the prone martyr's remains!

The drowning hero sprang up with a relieving snort; there was a whiz as of a missile in the air, mingled with the murmur of a curse, a sound as of shivering glass followed, and a small vague form went over the fence and shot away in the gloom.

Huckleberry Finn

Monday came and, on his way to school, Tom came upon the juvenile pariah of the village, Huckleberry Finn, son of the town drunkard. Huckleberry was cordially hated and dreaded by all the mothers of the town becausd he was idle, and lawless, and vulgar.

"Hello, Huckleberry!"

"Hello yourself, and see how you like it!"

"What's that you got?"

"Dead cat."

"Lemme see him, Huck. My, he's pretty stiff. Where'd you get him?"

"Bought him off'n a boy."

"What did you give?"

"I give a blue ticket and a bladder that I got at the slaughter house."

"Where'd you get the blue ticket?"

"Bought it off'n Ben Rogers two weeks ago for a hoopstick."

"Say—what is dead cats good for, Huck?"

"Good for? Cure warts with."

"How do you cure 'em with dead cats?"

"Why, you take your cat and go and get in the graveyard, long about midnight, where somebody that was wicked has been buried. When it's midnight a devil will come, or maybe two or three, but you can't see 'em, you can only hear something like the wind, or maybe hear 'em talk; and when they're taking that feller away you heave your cat after 'em and say, 'Devil follow corpse, cat follow devil, warts follow cat. I'm done with ye!' That'll fetch any wart."

"Sounds right. D'you ever try it, Huck?"

"No, but old Mother Hopkins told me."

"Well, I reckon it's so, then, becuz they say she's a witch."

"Say! Why, Tom, I know she is. She witched Pap. Pap says so his own self. He came along one day, and he see she was a witching him, so he took up a rock, and if she hadn't dodged he'd a got her. Well, that very night he rolled off'n a shed wher' he was a layin' drunk, and broke his arm."

"Why that's awful. How did he know she was a witching him?"

"Lord, Pap can tell, easy. Pap says when they keep looking at you right stiddy, they're a witching you, specially if they mumble. Becuz when they mumble they're a saying the Lord's Prayer backwards."

"Say, Hucky, when you going to try the cat?"

"Tonight. I reckon they'll come after old Hoss Williams tonight."

"But they buried him Saturday, Huck. Didn't they get him Saturday night?"

"Why, how you talk! How could their charms work till midnight and then it's Sunday? Devils don't slosh around much of a Sunday, I don't reckon."

"I never thought of that. Lemme go with you?"

"Of course—if you ain't afeard."

"Afeard! 'Tain't likely. Will you meow?"

"Yes, and you meow back if you get a chance. Last time you kep' me a meowing around till old Hays sent to throwing rocks at me, and says, 'Dern that cat!' So I hove a brick through his window— but don't you tell."

"I won't. I couldn't meow that night becuz Auntie was watching me; but I'll meow this time."

School

When Tom reached the little isolated frame school-house, he strode in briskly, with the manner of one who had come with all honest speed. He hung his hat on a peg, and flung himself into his seat with businesslike alacrity. The master, throned on high in his great splint-bottom armchair, was dozing, lulled by the frowsy hum of study. The interruption roused him:

"Thomas Sawyer!"

Tom knew that when his name was pronounced in full, it meant trouble.

"Sir!"

"Come up here. Now, sir, why are you late again, as usual?"

Tom was about to take refuge in a lie, when he saw two long tails of yellow hair hanging down a back that he recognised by the electric sympathy of love; and by that form was the only vacant place on the girl's side of the school-house. He instantly said:

"I STOPPED TO TALK WITH HUCKLEBERRY FINN!"

The master's pulse stood still, and he stared helplessly. The buzz of study ceased; the pupils wondered if this fool-hardy boy had lost his mind. The master said:

"You—you did what?"

"Stopped to talk with Huckleberry Finn."

There was no mistaking the words.

"Thomas Sawyer, this is the most astounding

confession I have ever listened to; no mere ferule will answer for this offence. Take off your jacket."

The master's arm performed until it was tired, and the stock of switches notably diminished. Then the order followed:

"Now, sir, go and sit with the girls! And let this be a warning to you."

The titter that rippled around the room appeared to abash the boy, but in reality that result was caused rather more by his worshipful awe of his unknown idol and the dread pleasure that lay in his high good fortune. He sat down upon the end of the pine bench, and the girl hitched herself away from him with a toss of the head. Nudges, winks and whispers traversed the room, but Tom sat still, with his arms upon the long, low desk before him, and seemed to study his book. By and by attention ceased from him, and the accustomed school murmur rose upon the dull air once more.

Becky Thatcher

Presently the boy began to steal furtive glances at the girl. She observed it, 'made a mouth' at him, and gave him the back of her head for the space of a minute. When she cautiously faced around again, a peach lay before her. She thrust it away; Tom gently put it back; she thrust it away again, but with less animosity. Tom scrawled on his slate, 'Please take it —I got more.' The girl glanced at the words, but made no sign. Now the boy began to draw something on the slate, hiding his work with his left hand. For a time the girl refused to notice; but her human curiosity presently began to manifest itself by hardly perceptible signs. The boy worked on, apparently unconscious. The girl made a sort of non-committal attempt to see, but the boy did not betray that he was aware of it. At last she gave in, and hesitatingly whispered:

"Let me see it."

Tom partly uncovered a dismal caricature of a house with two gable ends to it and a cork-screw of smoke issuing from the chimney. Then the girl's interest began to fasten itself upon the work, and she forgot everything else. When it was finished, she gazed a moment, then she whispered:

"It's nice—make a man."

The artist erected a man in the front yard, that resembled a derrick. He could have stepped over the house; but the girl was not hypercritical; she was satisfied with the monster, and whispered:

"It's a beautiful man—now make me coming along."

Tom drew an hourglass, with a full moon and straw limbs to it, and armed the spreading fingers with a portentous fan. The girl said:

"It's ever so nice—I wish I could draw."

"It's easy," whispered Tom. "I'll learn you."

"Oh, will you? When?"

"At noon. Do you go home to dinner?"

"I'll stay if you will."

"Good—that's a go."

"What's your name?"

"Becky Thatcher."

"What's yours? Oh, I know. It's Thomas Sawyer."

"That's the name they lick me by. I'm Tom when I'm good. You call me Tom, will you?"

"Yes."

Now Tom began to scrawl something on the slate, hiding the words from the girl. But she was not backward this time. She begged to see. Tom said:

"Oh, it ain't anything."

"Yes it is."

"No it ain't; you don't want to see."

"Yes I do, indeed I do. Please let me."

"You'll tell."

"No I won't—deed and deed and double deed I won't."

"You won't tell anybody at all? Ever as long as you live?"

"No, I won't ever tell anybody. Now let me."

"Oh, you don't want to see!"

"Now that you treat me so I will see, Tom"—and she put her small hand on his, and a little scuffle ensued. Tom pretending to resist in earnest, but letting his hand slip by degrees till these words were revealed: 'I love you.'

"Oh you bad thing!" And she hit his hand a smart rap, but reddened and looked pleased nevertheless.

Just at this juncture the boy felt a slow fateful grip closing on his ear, and a steady lifting impulse. In that vice he was borne across the house and deposited in his own seat, under a peppering fire of giggles from the whole school. Then the master stood over him during a few awful moments, and finally moved away to his throne without saying a word. But although Tom's ear tingled, his heart was jubilant.

As the school quieted down, Tom made an honest effort to study, but the turmoil within him was too great. In turn he took his place in the reading class and made a botch of it, then in the geography class and turned lakes into mountains, mountains into rivers, and rivers into continents, till chaos was come again; then in the spelling class, and got 'turned down' by a succession of mere baby words till he brought up at the foot and yielded up the pewter

Secret Meeting

So the one went off with one group of scholars, and the other with another. In a little while the two met at the bottom of the lane, and when they reached the school they had it all to themselves. Then they sat together, with a slate before them, and Tom gave Becky the pencil and held her hand in his, guiding it, and so created another surprising house. When the interest in art began to wane, the two fell to talking. Tom was swimming in bliss. He said:

"Do you love rats?"

"No, I hate them!"

"Well, I do too—live ones. But I mean dead ones, to swing around your head with a string."

"No, I don't care for rats much, anyway. What I like is chewing gum!"

"Oh, I should say so! I wish I had some now!"

"Do you? I've got some. I'll let you chew it awhile, but you must give it back to me."

That was agreeable, so they chewed it turn about, and dangled their legs against the bench in excess of contentment.

"Was you ever at a circus?" said Tom.

"Yes, and my pa's going to take me again sometime, if I'm good."

"I been to the circus three or four times—lots of times. Church ain't shucks to a circus. There's things going on at a circus all the time. I'm going to be a clown in a circus when I grow up."

"Oh, are you? That will be nice. They're so lovely all spotted up."

"Yes, that's so. And they get slathers of money—

medal which he had worn with ostentation for months.

When school broke up at noon, Tom flew to Becky Thatcher, and whispered in her ear.

"Put on your bonnet and let on you're going home; and when you get to the corner, give the rest of 'em the slip, and turn down through the lane and come back. I'll go the other way, and come it over 'em the same way."

most a dollar a day, Ben Rogers says. Say, Becky, was you ever engaged?"

"What's that?"

"Why, engaged to be married."

"No."

"Would you like to?"

"I reckon so. I don't know. What is it like?"

"Like? Why it ain't like anything. You only just tell a boy you won't ever have anybody but him, ever, ever, ever, and then you kiss, and that's all. Anybody can do it."

"Kiss? What do you kiss for?"

"Why that, you know, is to—well, they always do that."

"Everybody?"

"Why, yes, everybody that's in love with each other. Do you remember what I wrote on the slate?"

"Ye—yes."

"What was it?"

"I shan't tell you."

"Shall I tell you?"

"Ye—yes—but some other time."

"No, now."

"No not now—tomorrow."

"Oh, no, now, please, Becky. I'll whisper it, I'll whisper it ever so easy."

Becky hesitating, Tom took silence for consent, and passed his arm about her waist and whispered the tale ever so softly, and with his mouth close to her ear, he added:

"Now you whisper it to me—just the same."

She resisted for a while, and then said:

"You turn your face away, so you can't see, and then I will. But you mustn't ever tell anybody—will you, Tom? Now you won't—will you?"

"No, indeed, indeed I won't. Now, Becky."

He turned his face away. She bent timidly around till her breath stirred his hair, and whispered, "I love you!"

Then she sprang away and ran around and around the desks and benches with Tom after her, and took refuge in a corner at last, with her little white apron to her face. Tom clasped her about her neck and pleaded.

"Now, Becky, it's all over—all over but the kiss. Don't you be afraid of that—it ain't anything at all. Please, Becky."

And he tugged at the apron and the hands.

By-and-by she gave up and let her hands drop; her face, all glowing with the struggle, came up and submitted. Tom kissed the red lips and said:

"Now it's all done, Becky. And always after this, you know, you ain't never to love anybody but me, and you ain't ever to marry anybody but me, never, never and for ever. Will you?"

"No, I'll never love anybody but you, Tom, and I'll never marry anybody but you, and you ain't to ever marry anybody but me, either."

"Certainly. Of course. That's part of it. And always, coming to school, or when we're going home, you're to walk with me, when there ain't anybody looking—and you choose me and I choose you at parties, because that's the way you do when you're engaged."

"It's so nice. I never heard of it before."

"Oh, it's ever so jolly! Why me and Amy Lawrence——"

The big eyes told Tom his blunder, and he stopped, confused.

"Oh, Tom! Then I ain't the first you've ever been engaged to!"

The child began to cry. Tom said:

"Oh, don't cry, Becky. I don't care for her any more."

"Yes you do, Tom—you know you do."

Tom tried to put his arm around her neck, but she pushed him away and turned her face to the wall, and went on crying. Tom tried again, with soothing words in his mouth, and was repulsed again. Then his pride was up, and he strode away and went outside. He stood about, restless and uneasy, for a while, glancing at the door every now and then, hoping she would repent and come to find him. But she did not. Then he began to feel badly, and fear that he was in the wrong. It was a hard struggle with him to make new advances now, but he nerved himself to it and entered. She was still standing back there in the corner, sobbing with her face to the wall. Tom's heart smote him. He went to her and stood for a moment, not knowing exactly what to say. Then he said, hesitatingly:

"Becky, I—I don't care for anybody but you."

No reply—but sobs.

"Becky," pleadingly, "Becky, won't you say something?"

More sobs.

Tom got out his chiefest jewel, a brass knob from the top of an endiron, and passed it around her so that she could see it, and said:

"Please, Becky, won't you take it?"

She struck it to the floor. Then Tom marched out of the house and over the hills and far away, to return to school no more that day. Presently Becky began to suspect. She ran to the door; he was not there. Then she called:

"Tom! Come back, Tom!"

She listened intently, but there was no answer. She had no companions but silence and loneliness.

So she sat down to cry again and upbraid herself. By this time the scholars began to gather again, and she had to hide her grief and still her broken heart, and take up the cross of a long dreary aching afternoon with none among the strangers about her to exchange sorrows with.

The Graveyard

At half past nine that night, Tom and Sid, his brother, were sent to bed as usual. They said their prayers, and Sid was soon asleep. Tom lay awake and waited in restless impatience. The raising of a neighbouring window disturbed him. A cry of 'Scat! you devil!' and the crash of an empty bottle against the back of his aunt's wood-shed brought him wide awake, and a single minute later he was dressed and out of the window and creeping along the roof of the 'ell' on all fours. He 'meow'd' with caution once or twice as he went; then jumped to the roof of the wood-shed, and thence to the ground. Huckleberry Finn was there, with his dead cat. The boys moved off and disappeared in the gloom. At the end of half an hour they were wading through the tall grass of the graveyard.

A faint wind moaned through the trees, and Tom

feared it might be the spirits of the dead complaining at being disturbed. The boys talked little, and only under their breath, for the time and the place and the pervading solemnity and silence oppressed their spirits. They found the sharp new heap they were seeking, and ensconced themselves within the protection of three great elms that grew in a bunch near to the grave.

Then they waited in silence for what seemed a long time. The hooting of a distant owl was all the sound that troubled the dead stillness. Tom's reflection grew oppressive. He must force some talk. So he said in a whisper:

"Hucky, do you believe the dead people like it for us to be here?"

Huckleberry whispered:

"I wisht I knowed. It's awful solemn like, ain't it?"

"I bet it is."

There was a considerable pause, while the boys canvassed this matter inwardly. Then Tom whispered:

"Say, Hucky—do you reckon Hoss Williams hears us talking?"

"O' course he does. Least his spirit does."

Tom, after a pause:

"I wish I'd said Mister Williams. But I never meant any harm. Everybody calls him Hoss."

"A body can't be too particular how they talk 'bout these yer dead people, Tom."

This was a damper, and conversation died again. Presently Tom seized his comrade's arm and said:

"Sh!"

"What is it, Tom?" And the two clung together with beating hearts.

"Sh! There 'tis again! Didn't you hear it?"

"I—"

"There! Now you hear it!"

"Lord, Tom, they're coming! They're coming, sure. What'll we do?"

"I dono. Think they'll see us?"

"Oh, Tom, they can see in the dark same as cats. I wish I hadn't come!"

"Oh, don't be afeard. I don't believe they'll bother us. We ain't doing any harm. If we keep perfectly still, maybe they won't notice us at all."

"I'll try to, Tom, but Lord, I'm all of a shiver."

"Listen!"

The boys bent their heads together and scarcely breathed. A muffled sound of voices floated up from the far end of the graveyard.

"Look! see there!" whispered Tom. "What is it?"

"It's devil-fire. Oh, Tom, this is awful."

Some vague figures approached through the gloom, swinging an old-fashioned tin lantern that freckled the ground with innumerable little spangles of light. Presently Huckleberry whispered with a shudder:

"It's the devils, sure enough. Three of 'em! Lordy, Tom, we're goners! Can you pray?"

"I'll try, but don't you be afeard. They ain't going to hurt us. 'Now I lay me down to sleep, I—'"

"Sh!"

"What is it, Huck?"

"They're humans! One of 'em is, anyway. One of 'em is old Muff Potter's voice."

"No—'tain't so, is it?"

"I bet I know it. Don't you stir nor budge. He ain't sharp enough to notice us."

"All right, I'll keep still. Now they're stuck. Can't find it. Here they come again. Now they're hot. Cold again. Hot again. Red-hot! They're pinted right, this time. Say, Huck, I know another o' them's voices; it's Injun Joe."

"That's so—that murderin' half-breed! I'd ruther they was devils a dern sight. What kin they be up to Tom?"

The whispers died wholly out now, for the three men had reached the grave, and stood a short distance from the boys' hiding-place.

"Hurry, men!" he said in a low voice. "The moon might come out at any moment!"

For some time there was no noise but the grating sound of the spades discharging their freight of mould and gravel. It was very monotonous. Finally a spade struck upon the coffin with a dull, woody accent, and within another minute or two the men had hoisted it out on the ground. They prised off the lid with their shovels, got out the body and dumped it rudely on the ground. The moon drifted from behind the clouds and exposed the pallid face. The barrow was got ready and the corpse placed on it, covered with a blanket, and bound to its place with the rope. Potter took out a large spring-knife and cut off the dangling end of the rope, and then said:

"Now the cussed thing's ready, Sawbones, and you'll just out with another five, or here she stays."

"That's the talk!" said Injun Joe.

"Look here; what does this mean?" said the doctor. "You required your pay in advance and I've paid you."

"Yes, and you done more than that," said Injun Joe, approaching the doctor, who was now standing. "Five years ago you drove me away from your father's kitchen one night when I come to ask for something to eat, and you said I warn't there for any good; and when I swore I'd get even with you if it took a hundred years, your father had me jailed for a vagrant. Did you think I'd forget? The Injun blood ain't in me for nothing. And now I've got you, and you got to settle you know!"

He was threatening the doctor with his fist in his face by this time. The doctor struck out suddenly, and stretched the ruffian on the ground. Potter dropped his knife, and exclaimed:

"Here, now, don't you strike my pard!" and the next moment he had grappled with the doctor, and the two were struggling with might and main, trampling the grass, and tearing the ground with their heels. Injun Joe sprang to his feet, his eyes flaming with passion, snatched up Potter's knife, and went creeping, catlike, and stooping round and round about the combatants, seeking an opportunity. Just as the doctor knocked Potter unconscious with a heavy blow, Injun Joe drove that knife to the hilt in the young man's breast. He reeled and fell partly upon Potter, flooding him with his blood, and in the same moment the clouds blotted out the dreadful spectacle, and the two frightened boys went speeding away in the dark.

The Grave Robbers

"Here it is," said the third voice; and the owner of it held the lantern up and revealed the face of young Dr Robinson.

Potter and Injun Joe were carrying a hand-barrow with a rope and a couple of shovels on it. They cast down their load and began to open the grave. The doctor put the lantern at the head of the grave, and came and sat down with his back against one of the elm-trees. He was so close the boys could have touched him.

Presently when the moon emerged again Injun Joe was standing over the two forms, contemplating them. The doctor murmured and gave a long gasp or two, and was still. The half-breed muttered:

"That score is settled, damn you."

Then he robbed the body. After which he put the fatal knife in Potter's open right hand, and sat down on the dismantled coffin. Three—four—five minutes passed, and then Potter began to stir and moan. His hand closed upon the knife, he raised it, glanced at it, and let it fall with a shudder. Then he sat up, pushing the body from him, and gazed at it and then around him confusedly. His eyes met Joe's.

"Lord, how is this, Joe?" he said.

"It's a dirty business," said Joe, without moving. "What did you do it for?"

"I! I never done it!"

"Look here! That kind of talk won't wash."

Potter trembled and grew white. "I thought I'd got sober. I'd no business to drink tonight. But it's in my head yet—worsen' when we started here. I'm all in a muddle; can't recollect anything of it hardly. Tell me, Joe—honest now, old feller—did I do it, Joe? I never meant to; 'pon my soul and honour I never meant to, Joe."

Two or three minutes later the murdered man, the blanketed corpse, the lidless coffin, and the open grave, were under no inspection but the moon's. The stillness was complete again, too.

Witness to Murder

The two boys flew on and on towards the village, speechless with horror. They glanced backward and from time to time as if they feared they might be followed.

"If we can only get to the old tannery before we break down!" whispered Tom, in short catches between breaths. "I can't stand it much longer."

Huckleberry's hard pantings were his only reply, and the boys fixed their eyes on the goal of their hopes, and bent to their work to win it. They gained steadily on it, and at last, breast to breast, they burst in through the open door, and fell, grateful and exhausted, in the sheltering shadows beyond. By and by their pulses slowed down, and Tom whispered:

"Huck, what do you reckon'll come of this?"

"If Dr Robinson dies, I reckon hangin'll come of it."

"Do you, though?"

"Why, I know it, Tom."

Tom thought awhile; then he said:

"Who'll tell? We?"

"What are you talking about? S'pose something happened and Injun Joe didn't hang, why he'd kill us some time or other, just as dead sure as we're a lying here."

"That's just what I was thinking to myself, Huck!"

"If anybody tells, let Muff Potter do it, if he's fool enough. He's generally drunk enough."

Tom said nothing—went on thinking. Presently he whispered:

"Huck, Muff Potter don't know it. How can he tell?"

"What's the reason he don't know it?"

"Because he'd just got that whack when Injun Joe done it. D'you reckon he could see anything? D'you reckon he knowed anything?"

"By hokey, that's so, Tom!"

"And besides, look-a-here—maybe that whack done for him!"

"No, 'tain't likely, Tom. He had liquor in him; I could see that; and besides, he always has. Well, when Pap's full, you might take and belt him over the head with a church and you couldn't phase him. He says so his own self. So it's the same with Muff Potter, of course. But if a man was dead sober, I reckon, maybe that whack might fetch him; I dono."

After another reflective silence, Tom said:

"Hucky, you sure you can keep mum?"

"Tom, we got to keep mum. You know that. That Injun devil wouldn't make any more of drownding us than a couple of cats, if we was to squeak 'bout this and they didn't hang him. Now look-a-here, Tom, less take and swear to one another—that's what we got to do—swear to keep mum."

"Yes, I reckon that's so."

They continued to whisper for some little time. Presently a dog set up a long, low howl just outside —fairly near to them. The boys clasped each other suddenly, in an agony of fright. Then Tom, looking through a crack, exclaimed:

"Oh, Huck, it's a stray dog!"

"Quick, Tom, quick! Who does he mean?"

"Huck, he must mean us both—we're right together."

Tom choked off and whispered:

"Look, Hucky, look! He's got his back to us!"

Hucky looked with joy in his heart.

"Well, he has, by jingoes! Did he before?"

"Yes, he did. But I, like a fool, never thought. Oh, this is bully, you know. Now, who can he mean?"

The howling stopped. Tom pricked up his ears.

"Sh! What's that?" he whispered.

"Sounds like—like hogs grunting. No—it's somebody snoring, Tom."

"That is it? Where'bouts is it, Huck?"

"I b'leeve it's down at t'other end. Sounds so, anyway."

"Hucky, do you das't go if I lead?"

"I don't like to, much, Tom. S'pose it's Injun Joe!"

Tom quailed. But presently the temptation rose up strong and the boys agreed to try, with the understanding that they would take to their heels if the snoring stopped. So they went tip-toeing stealthily down, the one behind the other. When they had got to within five steps of the snorer, Tom stepped on a stick, and it broke with a sharp snap. The man moaned, writhed a little, and his face came into the moonlight. It was Muff Potter. The boys' hearts had stood still, and their bodies too, when the man moved, but their fears passed away now. They tiptoed out, through the broken weather boarding, and stopped at a little distance to exchange a parting word. That long, lugubrious howl rose on the night air again! They turned and saw the strange dog standing close to where Potter was lying, and facing Potter with his nose pointing heaven-ward. Then they separated.

When Tom crept in at his bedroom window, the night was almost spent. He undressed with excessive caution, and fell asleep congratulating himself that nobody knew of his escapade.

Muff Potter Accused

Close upon the hour of noon the whole village was suddenly electrified with the ghastly news. A gory knife had been found close to the murdered man, and it had been recognised by somebody as belonging to Muff Potter—so the story ran. And it was said that a belated citizen had come upon Potter washing himself in the 'branch' about one or two o'clock in the morning, and that Potter had at once sneaked off – suspicious circumstances, especially the washing, which was not a habit with Potter. It was also said that the town had been ransacked for this 'murderer' (the public are not slow in the matter of sifting evidence and arriving at a verdict), but that he could not be found. Horsemen had departed down all the roads in every direction, and the Sheriff was confident that he would be captured before night.

All the town was drifting towards the graveyard. Tom joined the procession, not because he would not a thousand times rather go anywhere else, but because an awful fascination drew him on. Arrived at the dreadful place, he wormed his small body through the crowd and saw the dismal spectacle. It seemed to him an age since he was there before. Somebody pinched his arm. He turned, and his eyes met Huckleberry's. Then both looked elsewhere at once, and wondered if anybody had noticed anything in their mutual glance. But everybody was talking, and intent upon the grisly spectacle before them.

"Poor fellow!" "Poor young fellow!" "This ought to be a lesson to grave-robbers!" "Muff Potter'll hang for this if they catch him!" This was the drift of remark, and the minister said, "It was a judgement; His hand is here."

Now Tom shivered from head to heel; for his eye fell upon the stolid face of Injun Joe. At this moment the crowd began to sway and struggle, and voices shouted, 'It's him! It's him! He's coming himself!'

"Who? Who?" from twenty voices.

"Muff Potter!"

"Hallo, he's stopped! Look out, he's turning! Don't let him get away!"

People in the branches of the trees over Tom's head said he wasn't trying to get away—he only looked doubtful and perplexed.

"Infernal impudence!" said a bystander; "wanted to come and take a quiet look at his work—didn't expect any company."

The crowd fell apart now, and the Sheriff came through ostentatiously, leading Potter by the arm.

The poor fellow's face was haggard, and his eyes showed the fear that was upon him. When he stood before the murdered man, he shook as with a palsy, and he put his face in his hands and burst into tears.

"I didn't do it, friends," he sobbed; "'pon my word and honour I never done it."

"Who's accused you?" shouted a voice.

This shot seemed to carry home. Potter lifted his face and looked around him with a pathetic hopelessness in his eyes. He saw Injun Joe, and exclaimed:

"Oh, Injun Joe, you promised me you'd never—"

"Is that your knife?" and it was thrust before him by the Sheriff.

Potter would have fallen if they had not caught him and eased him to the ground. Then he said:

"Something told me 't if I didn't come back and get——" He shuddered; then waved his nerveless hand with a vanquished gesture and said, "Tell 'em, Joe, tell 'em——it ain't no use any more."

Then Huckleberry and Tom stood dumb and staring, and heard the stony-hearted liar reel off his serene statement. They expecting every moment that the clear sky would deliver God's lightnings upon his head, and wondering to see how long the stroke was delayed. And when he had finished and still stood alive and whole, their wavering impulse to break their oath and save the poor betrayed prisoner's life faded and vanished away, for plainly this miscreant had sold himself to Satan, and it would be fatal to meddle with the property of such a power as that.

"Why didn't you leave? What did you want to come here for?" somebody said.

"I couldn't help it—I couldn't help it," Potter moaned. "I wanted to run away, but I couldn't seem to come anywhere but here." And he fell to sobbing again.

Injun Joe repeated his statement, a few minutes afterwards on the inquest, under oath, and helped to raise the body of the murdered man, and put it in a wagon for removal; and it was whispered through the shuddering crowd that the wound bled a little! The boys thought that this happy circumstance would turn suspicion in the right direction, but they were disappointed, for more than one villager remarked:

"It was very close to Muff Potter when it done it."

Tom's Conscience

Tom's fearful secret and gnawing conscience disturbed his sleep for as much as a week after this; and at breakfast one morning Sid said:

"Tom, you pitch around and talk in your sleep so much that you keep me awake about half the time."

Tom blanched and dropped his eyes.

"It's a bad sign," said Aunt Polly, gravely. "What you got on your mind, Tom?"

"Nothing. Nothing 't I know of." But the boy's hand shook so that he spilled his coffee.

"And you do talk such stuff," Sid said. "Last night you said, 'It's blood, it's blood, that's what it is!' You said that over and over. And you said, 'Don't torment me so—I'll tell.' Tell what?"

Everything was swimming before Tom. There is no telling what might have happened now, but luckily the concern passed out of Aunt Polly's face, and she came to Tom's relief without knowing it. She said:

"Sho! It's that dreadful murder. I dream about it most every night myself. Sometimes I dream it's me that done it."

Tom's sister, Mary, said she had been affected much the same way. Sid seemed satisfied. Tom got out of their presence as quickly as he plausibly could, and after that he complained of toothache for a week, and tied up his jaws every night. He never knew that Sid lay nightly watching, and frequently slipped the bandage free, and then leaned on his elbow listening a good while at a time, and afterwards slipped the bandage back in its place again. Tom's distress of mind wore off gradually, and the toothache grew irksome and was discarded. If Sid really managed to make anything out of Tom's mutterings, he kept it to himself. It seemed to Tom that his schoolmates never would get done holding inquests on dead cats, and thus keeping his trouble present to his mind. Sid noticed that Tom never was coroner at one of these inquiries, though it had been his habit to take the lead in all new enterprises; he noticed, too, that Tom never acted as a witness—and that was strange; and Sid did not overlook the fact that Tom even showed a marked aversion to these inquests, and always avoided them when he could. Sid marvelled, but said nothing. However, even inquests went out of vogue at last, and ceased to torture Tom's conscience.

Every day or two during this time of sorrow, Tom watched his opportunity and went to the little grated jail window and smuggled such small comforts through to the 'murderer' as he could get hold of. The jail was a trifling little brick den that stood in a marsh at the edge of the village, and no guards were afforded for it; indeed, it was seldom occupied. These offerings greatly helped to ease Tom's conscience. The villagers had a strong desire to tar and feather Injun Joe and ride him on a rail for body-snatching, but so formidable was his character that nobody could be found who was willing to take the lead in the matter, so it was dropped. He had been careful to begin both of his inquest statements with the fight, without confessing the grave-robbery that preceded it; therefore it was deemed wisest not to try the case in the courts at present.

Running Away from Home

One morning Tom awoke and wondered where he was. He sat up, rubbed his eyes and looked around; then he comprehended. It was the cool grey dawn, and there was a delicious sense of repose and peace in the deep pervading calm and silence of the woods. For he, Joe Harper and Huck had decided to run away from home and become pirates on Jackson Island.

Tom stirred up the others and they all clattered away with a shout, and in a minute or two were stripped and chasing after and tumbling over each other in the shallow limpid water of the white sand-bar. They felt no longing for the little village sleeping in the distance beyond the majestic waste of water. A vagrant current or a slight rise in the river had carried off their raft, but this only gratified them, since its going was something like burning the bridge between them and civilization.

They found plenty of things to be delighted with, but nothing to be astonished at. They discovered that the island was about three miles long and a quarter of a mile wide, and that the shore it lay closest to was only separated from it by a narrow channel. They took a swim about every hour, so it was close upon the middle of the afternoon when they got back to camp. They were too hungry to stop to fish, but they fared sumptuously upon cold ham, brought from home, and then threw themselves down in the shade to talk. But the talk soon began to drag, and then died. The stillness, the solemnity, that brooded in the woods, and the sense of loneliness, began to tell upon the spirits of the boys. They fell to thinking. A sort of undefined longing crept upon them. This took dim shape presently—it was budding homesickness. Even Finn the Red-handed (his new pirate name) was dreaming of his door-steps and empty hogsheads. But they were all ashamed of their weakness, and none was brave enough to speak his thought.

For some time now, the boys had been dully conscious of a peculiar sound in the distance, just as one sometimes is of the ticking of a clock which he takes no distinct note of. But now this mysterious sound became more pronounced, and forced a recognition. The boys started, glanced at each other, and then each assumed a listening attitude. There was a long silence, profound and unbroken; then a deep, sullen boom came floating down out of the distance.

"What is it?" exclaimed Joe, under his breath.

"I wonder," said Tom in a whisper.

"Tain't thunder," said Huckleberry, in an awed tone, "becuz thunder——"

"Hark!" said Tom; "listen—don't talk."

They waited a time that seemed an age, and then

the same muffled boom troubled the solemn hush.

"Let's go and see."

They sprang to their feet and hurried to the shore towards the town. They parted the bushes on the bank and peered out over the water. The little steam ferry-boat was about a mile below the village, drifting with the current. Her broad deck seemed crowded with people. There were a great many skiffs rowing about or floating with the stream in the neighbourhood of the ferry-boat, but the boys could not determine what the men in them were doing. Presently a great jet of white smoke burst from the ferry-boat's side, and as it expanded and rose in a lazy cloud, that same dull throb of sound was borne to the listeners again.

"I know now!" exclaimed Tom; "somebody's drownded!"

"That's it," said Huck; "they done that last summer when Bill Turner got drownded; they shoot a cannon over the water, and that makes him come up to the top."

"By jingo, I wish I was over there now," said Joe.

"I do too," said Huck. "I'd give heaps to know who it is."

The boys still listened and watched. Presently a revealing thought flashed through Tom's mind, and he exclaimed:

"Boys, I know who's drownded: it's us!"

They felt like heroes in an instant. Here was a gorgeous triumph; they were missed; they were mourned; hearts were breaking on their account; tears were being shed; accusing memories of unkindness to these poor lost lads were rising up, and unavailing regrets and remorse were being indulged. Best of all, the departed were the talk of the whole town, and the envy of all the boys, as far as this dazzling notoriety was concerned. This was fine. It was worth while to be a pirate, after all.

As twilight drew on, the ferry-boat went back to her accustomed business and the skiffs disappeared. The pirates returned to camp. They caught fish, cooked supper, and ate it, and then fell to guessing at what the village was thinking and saying about them.

As the night deepened, Huck began to nod, and presently to snore; Joe followed next. Tom lay upon his elbow motionless for some time, watching the two intently. At last he got up cautiously on his knees, and went searching among the grass and the flickering reflections flung by the camp-fire. He

picked up and inspected several large semi-cylinders of the thin white bark of a sycamore and finally chose two which seemed to suit him. Then he knelt by the fire and painfully wrote something upon each of these with his 'red keel'; one he rolled up and put in his jacket-pocket, and the other he put in Joe's hat and removed it to a little distance from the owner. And he also put into the hat certain schoolboy treasures of almost inestimable value, among them a lump of chalk, an india-rubber ball, three fish hooks, and one of that kind of marbles known as a 'sure 'nough crystal'. Then he tip-toed his way cautiously among the trees till he felt that he was out of hearing, and straightaway broke into a keen run in the direction of the sand-bar.

Tom's Escapade

A few minutes later Tom was in the shoal water of the bar, wading towards the Illinois shore. Before the depth reached his middle he was half-way over: the current would permit no more wading now, so he struck out confidently to swim the remaining distance. He reached the shore finally, and drifted along till he found a low place and drew himself out. He put his hand on his jacket pocket, found his piece of bark safe, and then struck through the woods, following the shore with streaming garments. Shortly before ten o'clock he came out into an open place opposite the village, and saw the ferry-boat lying in the shadow of the trees and the high bank.

Everything was quiet under the blinking stars. He crept down the bank, watching with all his eyes, slipped into the water, swam three or four strokes, and climbed into the skiff that did 'yawl' duty at the boat's stern. He laid himself down under the thwarts and waited, panting. Presently the cracked bell tapped, and a voice gave the order to 'cast off'. A minute or two later the skiff's head was standing high up against the boat's swell, and the voyage was begun. Tom felt happy in his success, for he knew it was the boat's last trip for the night. At the end of a long twelve or fifteen minutes the wheels stopped, and Tom slipped overboard and swam ashore in the dusk, landing a short distance down stream, out of danger of possible stragglers. He flew along unfre-quented alleys, and shortly found himself at his aunt's back fence. He climbed over, approached the 'ell' and looked in at the sitting room window, for a light was burning there. There sat Aunt Polly, Sid and Mary and Joe Harper's mother, grouped together, talking. They were by the bed, and the bed was between them and the door. Tom went to the door and began to softly lift the latch; then he pressed gently and the door yielded a crack; he continued pushing cautiously, and quaking every time it creaked, till he judged he might squeeze through on his knees; and so he put his head through and began, warily.

"What makes the candle blow so?" said Aunt Polly. Tom hurried up. "Why, that door's open, I believe. Why, of course it is. No end of strange things now. Go along and shut it, Sid."

Tom disappeared under the bed just in time. He lay and 'breathed' himself for a time, and then crept to where he could almost touch his aunt's foot as she resumed her conversation.

"But as I was saying," said Aunt Polly, "he warn't bad, so to say—only mischeevous. Only just giddy, and harum-scarum, you know. He warn't any more responsible than a colt. He never meant any harm, and he was the best-hearted boy that ever was"—and she began to cry.

"It was just so with my Joe—always full of his devilment, and up to every kind of mischief, but he was just as unselfish and kind as he could be—and, laws bless me, to think I went and whipped him for taking that cream, never once recollecting that I throwed it out myself because it was sour, and I never to see him again in this world, never, never, never, poor abused boy!" Mrs Harper sobbed as if her heart would break.

Tom stayed listening until Mrs Harper gave a sobbing good night and turned to go. Then with a mutual impulse the two bereaved women flung themselves into each other's arms and had a good consoling cry, and then parted. Aunt Polly was tender far beyond her wont in her good night to Sid and Mary. Sid snuffled a bit, and Mary went off crying with all her heart.

Aunt Polly knelt down and prayed for Tom so touchingly, so appealingly, and with such meas-ureless love in her words and her old trembling voice, that he was weltering in tears again long before she was through.

He had to keep still long after she went to bed, for

she kept making broken-hearted ejaculations from time to time, tossing unrestfully, and turning over. But at last she was still, only moaning a little in her sleep. Now the boy stole out, rose gradually by the bedside, shaded the candle-light with his hand, and stood regarding her. His heart was full of pity for her. He took out his sycamore scroll and placed it by the candle. But something occurred to him, and he lingered considering. His face lighted with a happy solution of his thought; he put the bark hastily in his pocket, then he bent over and kissed the faded lips, and straightway made his stealthy exit, latching the door behind him.

He threaded his way back to the ferry landing, untied the skiff at the stern, slipped into it, and was soon rowing up-stream. When he had pulled a mile above the village, he started across and bent himself stoutly to his work. He hit the landing on the other side neatly, for this was a familiar bit of work to him. He was moved to capture the skiff, arguing that it might be considered a ship and therefore legitimate prey for a pirate; but he knew a thorough search would be made for it, and that might end in revelations. So he stepped ashore and entered the wood. He sat down and took a long rest, torturing himself meantime to keep awake, and then started wearily down the home stretch. The night was far spent. It was broad daylight before he found himself fairly abreast the island bar. He rested again until the sun was well up and gilding the great river with its splendour, and then he plunged into the stream. A little later he paused, dripping, upon the threshold of the camp, and heard Joe say:

"No, Tom's true-blue, Huck, and he'll come back. He won't desert. He knows that would be a disgrace to a pirate, and Tom's too proud for that sort of thing. He's up to something or other. Now, I wonder what?"

"Well, the things is ours anyway, ain't they?"

"Pretty near, but not yet, Huck. The writing says they are if he ain't back to breakfast."

"Which he is!" exclaimed Tom, with fine dramatic effect, stepping grandly into camp.

A sumptuous breakfast of bacon and fish was shortly provided, and as the boys set to work upon it Tom recounted (and adorned) his adventures. They were a vain and boastful company of heroes when the tale was done. Then Tom hid himself away in a shady spot to sleep till noon, and the other pirates got ready to fish and explore.

The Unusual Funeral Sermon

But there was no hilarity in the little town that tranquil afternoon. The Harpers and Aunt Polly's family were being put into mourning with great grief and many tears. An unusual quiet possessed the village, although it was ordinarily quiet enough in all conscience. The villagers conducted their concerns with an abstracted air, and talked little; but they sighed often. The Saturday holiday seemed a burden to the children. They had no heart in their sports, and gradually gave them up.

When the Sunday-school hour was finished the next morning, the bell began to toll, instead of ringing in the usual way. It was a very still Sabbath, and the mournful sound seemed in keeping with the musing hush that lay upon nature. The villagers began to gather, loitering a moment in the vestibule to converse in whispers about the sad event. But there was no whispering in the house; only the funereal rustling of dresses, as the women gathered to their seats, disturbed the silence there. None could remember when the little church had been so full before. There was finally a waiting pause, an expectant dumbness, and then Aunt Polly entered, followed by Sid and Mary, and then by the Harper family, all in deep black. The whole congregation, the old minister as well, rose reverently and stood, until the mourners were seated in the front pew. There was another silence, broken by sobs, then the minister spread his hands abroad and prayed. A moving hymn was sung, and the text followed: "I am the resurrection and the life."

As the service proceeded, the clergyman drew such pictures of the graces, the winning ways, and the rare promise of the lost lads, that every soul there, thinking he recognized these pictures, felt a pang in remembering that he had persistently blinded himself to them always before; and had as persistently seen only faults and flaws in the poor boys. The minister related many a touching incident in the lives of the departed, too, which illustrated their sweet, generous natures, and the people could easily see, now, how noble and beautiful those episodes were, and remembered with grief that at the time they occurred they had seemed rank rascalities, well deserving the cowhide. The congregation became more and more moved as the pathetic tale went on, till at last the whole company broke down and joined the weeping mourners in a chorus of anguished sobs, the preacher himself giving way to his feelings, and crying in the pulpit.

There was a rustle in the gallery which nobody noticed; a moment later the church door creaked; the minister raised his streaming eyes above his handkerchief, and stood transfixed! First one and then another pair of eyes followed the minister's, and then, almost with one impulse, the congregation rose and stared while the three dead boys came marching up the aisle, Tom in the lead, Joe next, and Huck, a ruin of drooping rags, sneaking sheepishly in the rear. They had been hid in the unused gallery, listening to their own funeral sermon!

Aunt Polly, Mary and the Harpers threw themselves upon their restored ones, smothered them with kisses and poured out thanksgivings, while poor Huck stood abashed and uncomfortable, not knowing exactly what to do or where to hide from so many unwelcoming eyes. He wavered, and started to slink away, but Tom seized him and said:

"Aunt Polly, it ain't fair. Somebody's got to be glad to see Huck."

"And so they shall! I'm glad to see him, poor motherless thing!" And the loving attentions Aunt Polly lavished upon him were the one thing capable of making him more uncomfortable than he was before.

Suddenly the minister shouted at the top of his voice:

" 'Praise God from whom all blessings flow'— SING!—and put your hearts in it!"

And they did. The "Old Hundred" hymn swelled up with a triumphant burst, and while it shook the rafters, Tom Sawyer the Pirate looked around upon the envying juveniles about him, and confessed in his heart that this was the proudest moment in his life.

As the "sold" congregation trooped out, they said they would almost be willing to be made ridiculous again to hear Old Hundred sung like that once more.

Tom got more cuffs and kisses that day—according to Aunt Polly's varying moods—than he had earned before in a year; and he hardly knew which expressed the most gratefulness to God and affection for himself.

The Murder Trial

Time passed and at last the sleepy atmosphere was stirred, and vigorously. The murder trial came on in the court. It became the absorbing topic of village talk immediately. Tom and Huck did as they had often done before—went to the cell grating and gave Potter some tobacco and matches. He was on the ground floor, and there were no guards.

Muff Potter's gratitude for their gifts had always smote their consciences before—it cut deeper than ever, this time. They felt cowardly and treacherous to the last degree when Potter said:

"You've been mighty good to me, boys—better'n anybody else in this town. And I don't forget it, I don't. Often I says to myself, says I, 'I used to mend all the boys' kites and things, and show 'em where the good fishin' places was, and befriend 'em when I could, and now they've all forgot old Muff when he's in trouble, but Tom don't, and Huck don't—they don't forget him,' says I, and I don't forget them!"

All the village flocked to the court-house the next morning, for this was to be the great day. Both sexes were about equally represented in the packed audience. After a long wait the jury filed in and took their places; shortly afterwards, Potter, pale and haggard, timid and hopeless, was brought in with chains upon him, and seated where all the curious eyes could stare at him; no less conspicuous was Injun Joe, stolid as ever. There was another pause, and then the judge arrived, and the Sheriff proclaimed the opening of the court. The usual whisperings among the lawyers and gathering together of papers followed. These details and accompanying delays worked up an atmosphere of preparation that was as impressive as it was fascinating.

Every detail of the damaging circumstances that occurred in the graveyard upon that morning which all present remembered so well was brought out by credible witnesses, but none of them were cross-examined by Potter's lawyer. The perplexity and dissatisfaction of the house expressed itself in murmurs and provoked a reproof from the bench. Counsel for the prosecution now said:

"By the oaths of citizens whose simple word is above suspicion, we have fastened this awful crime beyond all possibility of question upon the unhappy prisoner at the bar. We rest our case here."

A groan escaped from poor Potter, and he put his face in his hands, and rocked his body softly to and fro, while a painful silence reigned in the courtroom. Many men were moved, and many women's compassion testified itself in tears. Counsel for the defence rose and said:

"Your Honour, in our remarks at the opening of this trial, we foreshadowed our purpose to prove that our client did this fearful deed while under the influence of a blind and irresponsible delirium produced by drink. We have changed our mind; we shall not offer that plea. (Then to the clerk.) Call Thomas Sawyer."

A puzzled amazement awoke in every face in the house, not even excepting Potter's. Every eye fastened itself with wondering interest upon Tom as he rose and took his place upon the stand. The boy looked wild enough, for he was badly scared. The oath was administered.

"Thomas Sawyer, where were you on the seventeenth of June, about the hour of midnight?"

Tom glanced at Injun Joe's face, and his tongue failed him. The audience listened breathless, but the words refused to come. After a few moments, however, the boy got a little of his strength back, and managed to put enough of it into his voice to make part of the house hear:

"In the graveyard!"

"A little bit louder, please. Don't be afraid. You were——"

"In the graveyard."

A contemptuous smile flitted across Injun Joe's face.

"Were you anywhere near Horse Williams's grave?"

"Yes, sir."

"Speak up just a trifle louder. How near were you?"

"Near as I am to you."

"Were you hidden or not?"

"I was hid."

"Where?"

"Behind the elms that's on the edge of the grave."

Injun Joe gave a barely perceptible start.

"Anyone with you?"

"Yes, sir. I went there with——"

"Wait—wait a moment. Never mind mentioning your companion's name. We will produce him at the proper time. Did you carry anything there with you?"

Tom hesitated and looked confused.

"Speak out, my boy—don't be diffident. The

truth is always respectable. What did you take there?"

"Only a—a—dead cat."

There was a ripple of mirth, which the court checked.

"We will produce the skeleton of that cat. Now my boy, tell us everything that occurred—tell it in your own way—don't skip anything, and don't be afraid."

Tom began—hesitatingly at first, but, as he warmed to his subject, his words flowed more and more easily; in a little while every sound ceased but his own voice; every eye fixed itself upon him; with parted lips and bated breath the audience hung upon

Tom the Hero

Tom was a glittering hero once more—the pet of the old, the envy of the young. His name even went into immortal print, for the village paper magnified him. There were some that believed he would be President yet, if he escaped hanging.

As usual, the fickle unreasoning world took Muff Potter to its bosom, and fondled him as lavishly as it had abused him before. But that sort of conduct is to the world's credit; therefore it is not well to find fault with it.

Tom's days were days of splendour and exultation to him, but his nights were seasons of horror. Injun Joe infested all his dreams, and always with doom in his eye. Hardly any temptation could persuade the boy to stir abroad after nightfall. Poor Huck was in the same state of wretchedness and terror, for Tom had told the whole story to the lawyer the night before the great day of the trial, and Huck was sore afraid that his share in the business might leak out as yet, notwithstanding Injun Joe's flight had saved him the suffering of testifying in court. The poor fellow had got the attorney to promise secrecy, but what of that? Since Tom's harassed conscience had managed to drive him to the lawyer's house by night and wring a dread tale from lips that had been sealed with the dismalest and most formidable of oaths, Huck's confidence in the human race was well-nigh obliterated.

Daily Muff Potter's gratitude made Tom glad he had spoken; but nightly he wished he had sealed up his tongue. Half the time Tom was afraid Injun Joe would never be captured; the other half he was afraid he would be. He felt sure he never could draw a safe breath again until that man was dead and he had seen the corpse with his own eyes.

Rewards had been offered, the country had been scoured, but no Injun Joe was found. One of those omniscient and awe-inspiring marvels, a detective, came up from St Louis, moused around, shook his head, looked wise, and made that sort of astounding success which members of that craft usually achieve. That is to say, 'he found a clue'. But you can't hang a 'clue' for murder, and so after the detective had got through and gone home, Tom felt just as insecure as he was before.

The slow days drifted on, and each left behind it a slightly lightened weight of apprehension as no news of Injun Joe was heard.

his words, taking no note of time, rapt in the ghastly fascinations of the tale. The strain upon pent emotion reached its climax when the boy said, "And as the doctor knocked Muff Potter out, Injun Joe jumped with the knife and——"

Crash! Quick as lightning, the half-breed sprang for a window, and was gone!

Treasure Hunting

There comes a time in every rightly constructed boy's life when he has a raging desire to go somewhere and dig for hidden treasure. This desire suddenly came upon Tom one day.

Presently he stumbled upon Huck Finn the Red-handed. Huck would answer. Tom took him to a private place, and opened the matter to him confidentially. Huck was willing. Huck was always willing to take a hand in any enterprise that offered entertainment and required no capital, for he had a troublesome super-abundance of that sort of time which is not money.

"Where'll we dig?" said Huck.

"Oh, 'most anywhere."

"Why, is it hid all around?"

"No, indeed it ain't. It's hid in mighty particular places, Huck. They always bury it under a ha'nted house, or on an island, or under a dead tree that's got one limb sticking out. Well, we've tried Jackson's Island a little, and we can try it again sometime; and there's the old ha'nted house up the Still-House branch and there's lots of dead-limb trees—dead loads of 'em."

"Is it under all of them?"

"How you talk! No!"

"Then how you going to know which one to go for?"

"Go for all of 'em."

"Why Tom, it'll take all summer."

"Well, what of that? Suppose you find a brass pot with a hundred dollars in it, all rusty and gay, or a rotten chest full of di'monds. How's that?"

After digging in a dozen places to no avail, Tom suggested they do some night digging.

"All right. Let's hide the tools in the bushes."

The boys were there that night about the appointed time. They sat in the shadow waiting. It was a lonely place, and an hour made solemn by old traditions. Spirits whispered in the rustling leaves, ghosts lurked in the murky nooks, the deep baying of a hound floated up out of the distance, an owl answered with his sepulchral note. The boys were subdued by these solemnities, and talked little. By-and-by they judged that twelve had come; they marked where the shadow fell and began to dig. Their hopes commenced to rise. Their interest grew stronger, and their industry kept pace with it. The hole deepened and still deepened, but every time their hearts jumped to hear the pick strike upon something, they only suffered a new disappointment. It was only a stone or a chunk. At last Tom said, "It ain't any use, Huck, we're wrong again."

"Say, Tom, let's give this place up, and try somewheres else."

"All right, I reckon we better."

"What'll it be?"

Tom considered awhile, and then said, "The ha'nted house. That's it."

"Well, all right. We'll tackle the ha'nted house if you say so; but I reckon it's taking chances."

Noon next day they reached the haunted house. There was something so weird and grisly about the dead silence that reigned there under the baking sun, and something so depressing about the loneliness and desolation of the place, that they were afraid, for a moment, to venture in. Then they crept to the door and took a trembling peep. They saw a weed-grown, floorless room, unplastered, an ancient fireplace, vacant windows, a ruinous staircase; and here, there, and everywhere, hung ragged and abandoned cobwebs. They presently entered softly, with quickened pulses, talking in whispers, ears alert to catch the slightest sound, and muscles tense and ready for instant retreat.

In a little while familiarity modified their fears, and they gave the place a critical and interested examination, rather admiring their own boldness, and wondering at it too. Next they wanted to look upstairs. This was something like cutting off retreat, but they got to daring each other, and of course there could be but one result—they threw their tools into a corner and made the ascent. Up there were the same signs of decay. In one corner they found a closet that promised mystery, but the promise was a fraud—there was nothing in it. Their courage was up now, and well in hand. They were about to go down and begin work when—

"Sh!" said Tom.

"What is it?" whispered Huck, blanching with fright.

"Sh! There! Hear it?"

"Yes! Oh, my! Let's run!"

"Keep still! Don't you budge! They're coming right towards the door."

The boys stretched themselves upon the floor with their eyes to knot-holes in the planking, and lay waiting in a misery of fear.

"They've stopped. No—coming. Here they are. Don't whisper another word, Huck. My goodness, I wish I was out of this!"

Injun Joe Turns Up Again

Two men entered. Each boy said to himself:

"There's the old deaf and dumb Spaniard that's been about town once or twice lately—never saw t'other man before."

'T'other' was a ragged, unkempt creature, with nothing very pleasant in his face. The Spaniard was wrapped in a serape; he had bushy white whiskers, long white hair flowed from under his sombrero, and he wore green goggles. When they came in, 't'other' was talking in a low voice; they sat down on the ground, facing the door, with their backs to the wall, and the speaker continued his remarks. His manner became less guarded and his words more distinct as he proceeded.

"No," said he, "I've thought it all over, and I don't like it. It's dangerous."

"Dangerous!" grunted the 'deaf and dumb' Spaniard, to the vast surprise of the boys. "Milksop!"

This voice made the boys gasp and quake. It was Injun Joe's! There was silence for some time. Then Injun Joe said:

"What's any more dangerous than the job up yonder—but nothing's come of it."

"That's different. Away up the river so, and not another house about. 'Twon't ever be known that we tried, anyway, long as we didn't succeed."

"Well, what's more dangerous than coming here in the daytime?—anybody would suspicion us that saw us."

"I know that. But there wasn't any other place as handy after that fool of a job. I want to quit this shanty. I wanted to yesterday only it wasn't any use trying to stir out of here with those infernal boys playing over there on the hill right in full view."

'Those infernal boys' quaked again under the inspiration of this remark, and thought how lucky it was that they had remembered it was Friday and concluded to wait a day. They wished in their hearts they had waited a year. The two men got out some food and made a luncheon. After a long and thoughtful silence Injun Joe said:

"Look here, lad, you go back up the river where you belong. Wait there till you hear from me. I'll take the chances on dropping into this town just once more, for a look. We'll do that 'dangerous' job after I've spied around a little and think things look well for it. Then for Texas! We'll leg it together!"

"Good idea," said the comrade, who walked

across the room, knelt down, raised one of the rearward hearth-stones and took out a bag that jingled pleasantly. He subtracted from it twenty or thirty dollars for himself and as much for Injun Joe, and passed the bag to the latter, who was on his knees in the corner, now, digging with his bowie-knife.

The boys forgot all their fears, all their miseries in an instant. With glaring eyes they watched every moment. Luck!— the splendour of it was beyond all imagination! There was money enough to make half a dozen boys rich! Here was treasure-hunting under the happiest auspices—there would not be any bothersome uncertainty as to where to dig. They nudged each other every moment—eloquent nudges and easily understood, for they simply meant, "Oh, but ain't you glad now we're here!"

Joe's knife struck upon something.

"Hello," said he.

"What is it?" said his comrade.

"Half-rotten plank—no, it's a box, I believe. Here, bear a hand, and we'll see what it's here for. Never mind, I've broke a hole."

He reached his hand in and drew it out.

"Man, it's money."

The two men examined the handful of coins. They were gold. The two boys above were as excited as themselves, and as delighted.

Joe's comrade said:

"We'll make quick work of this. There's an old rusty pick over amongst the weeds in the corner, the other side of the fire-place—I saw it a minute ago."

He ran and brought the boys' pick and shovel. Injun Joe took the pick, looked it over critically, shook his head, muttered something to himself, and then began to use it.

The box was soon unearthed. It was not very large; it was iron-bound and had been very strong before the slow years had injured it. The men contemplated the treasure awhile in blissful silence.

"Pard, there's thousands of dollars here," said Injun Joe.

" 'Twas always said that Murrel's gang used around here one summer," the stranger observed.

"I know it," said Injun Joe; "and this looks like it, I should say."

"Now you won't need to do that job."

The half-breed frowned. Said he:

"You don't know me. Least you don' know all about that thing. 'Tain't robbery altogether—it's

revenge!'' and a wicked light flamed in his eyes. "I'll need your help in it. When it's finished—then Texas. Go home to your Nance and your kids, and stand by till you hear from me."

"Well, if you say so. What'll we do with this—bury it again?"

"Yes. (ravishing delight overhead) No! by the great Sachem, no! (profound distress overhead) I'd nearly forgot. That pick had fresh earth on it! (The boys were sick with terror in a moment.) What business has a pick and a shovel here? What business with fresh earth on them? Who brought them here—and where are they gone? Have you heard anybody? Seen anybody? What! bury it again and leave them to come and see the ground disturbed? Not exactly—not exactly. We'll take it to my den."

"Why, of course! Might have thought of that before. You mean number one?"

"No—number two—under the cross. The other place is bad—too common."

"All right. It's nearly dark enough to start."

Injun Joe got up and went about from window to window, cautiously peeping out. Presently he said:

"Who could have brought those tools here? Do you reckon they can be upstairs?"

The boys' breath forsook them. Injun Joe put his hand on his knife, halted a moment, undecided, and then turned towards the stairway. The boys thought of the closet, but their strength was gone. The steps came creaking up the stairs—the intolerable distress of the situation woke the stricken resolution of the lads—they were about to spring for the closet, when there was a crash of rotten timbers, and Injun Joe landed on the ground amid the debris of the ruined stairway. He gathered himself up cursing, and his comrade said:

"Now what's the use of all that? If it's anybody, and they're up there, let them stay there—who cares? If they want to jump down, now, and get into trouble, who objects? It will be dark in fifteen minutes—and then let them follow us if they want to; I'm willing. In my opinion, whoever hove those things in here caught a sight of us, and took us for ghosts or devils. I'll bet they're running yet."

Joe grumbled awhile; then he agreed with his friend that what daylight was left ought to be economised in getting things ready for leaving. Shortly afterwards they slipped out of the house in the deepening twilight, and moved towards the river with their precious box.

Tracking Down Injun Joe

The adventure of the day mightily tormented Tom's dreams that night. But the incidents of his adventure grew sensibly sharper and clearer under the attrition of thinking them over, and so he presently found himself leaning to the impression that the thing might not have been a dream after all. This uncertainty must be swept away. He would snatch a hurried breakfast, and go and find Huck.

Huck was sitting on the gunwale of a flat boat, listlessly dangling his feet in the water, and looking very melancholy. Tom concluded to let Huck lead up to the subject. If he did not do it, then the adventure would be proved to have been only a dream.

"Hello, Huck!"

"Hello, yourself."

Silence for a minute.

"Tom, if we'd a left the blame tools at the dead tree we'd a got the money. Oh, ain't it awful!"

" 'Tain't a dream, then, 'tain't a dream! Somehow

I 'most wish it was. Dog'd if I don't.''

"What ain't a dream?"

"Oh, that thing yesterday. I ben half thinking it was.''

"Dream! If them stairs hadn't broke down you'd a seen how much a dream it was! I've had dreams enough all night, with that patch-eyed Spanish devil going for me all through 'em, rot him!''

"No, not rot him. Find him! Track the money!''

"Tom, we'll never find him. A feller don't only have one chance for such a pile, and that one's lost. I'd feel mighty shaky if I was to see him, anyway.''

"Well, so'd I; but I'd like to see him anyway, and track him out—to his number two.''

"Number two; yes, that's it. I ben thinking 'bout that. But I can't make nothing out of it. What do you reckon it is?''

"I dono. It's too deep. Say, Huck—maybe it's the number of a house!''

"Goody! No, Tom, that ain't it. If it is, it ain't in

this one-horse town. They ain't no numbers here."

"Well, that's so. Lemme think a minute. Here—it's the number of a room—in a tavern, you know!"

"Oh, that's the trick! They ain't only two taverns. We can find out quick."

"You stay here, Huck, till I come."

Tom was off at once. He did not care to have Huck's company in public places. He was gone half an hour. He found that in the best tavern, number two had long been occupied by a young lawyer, and was still so occupied. In the less ostentatious house number two was a mystery. The tavern-keeper's young son said it was kept locked all the time, and he never saw anybody go into it or come out of it except at night. He did not know any particular reason for this state of things, had had some little curiosity, but it was rather feeble; had made the most of the mystery by entertaining himself with the idea that the room was 'ha'nted'; had noticed that there was a light in there the night before.

"That's what I've found out, Huck. I reckon that's the very number two we're after."

"I reckon it is, Tom. Now what are you doing to do?"

"Lemme think."

Tom thought a long time. Then he said:

"I'll tell you. The back door of that number two is the door that comes out into that little close alley between the tavern and the old rattle-trap of a brick-store. Now you get hold of all the door keys you can find and I'll nip all of Auntie's, and the first dark night we'll go there and try 'em. And mind you keep a look out for Injun Joe, because he said he was going to drop into town and spy around once more for a chance to get his revenge. If you see him, you just follow him; and if he don't go to that number two, that ain't the place."

"Lordy, I don't want to foller him by myself!"

"Why, it'll be night, sure. He mightn't ever see you—and if he did, maybe he'd never think anything."

"Well, if it's pretty dark I reckon I'll track him. I dono—I dono. I'll try."

"You bet I'll follow him if it's dark, Huck! Why, he might a found out he couldn't get his revenge, and be going right after that money."

"It's so, Tom, it's so. I'll foller him; I will, by jingoes."

"Now you're talking! Don't you ever weaken, Huck, and I won't."

Finding Injun Joe

That night Tom and Huck were ready for their adventure. They hung about the neighbourhood of the tavern until after nine, one watching the alley at a distance and the other the tavern door. Nobody entered the alley or left it; nobody resembling the Spaniard entered or left the tavern door. The night promised to be a fair one; so Tom went home with the understanding that if a considerable degree of darkness came on, Huck was to come and 'meow', whereupon he would slip out and try the keys. But the night remained clear, and Huck closed his watch and retired to bed in an empty sugar hogshead about twelve.

Tuesday the boys had the same ill-luck. Also Wednesday. But Thursday night promised better. Tom slipped out in good season with his aunt's old tin lantern, and a large towel to blindfold it with. He hid the lantern in Huck's sugar hogshead and the watch began. An hour before midnight the tavern closed up, and its lights (the only ones thereabouts) were put out. No Spaniard had been seen. Nobody had entered or left the alley.

Tom got his lantern, lit it in the hogshead, wrapped it closely in the towel, and the two adventurers crept in the gloom towards the tavern. Huck stood sentry and Tom felt his way into the alley. Then there was a season of waiting anxiety that weighed upon Huck's spirits like a mountain. He began to wish he could see a flash from the lantern—it would frighten him, but it would at least tell him that Tom was alive yet.

It seemed hours since Tom had disappeared. Surely he must have fainted; maybe he was dead; maybe his heart had burst under terror and excitement. In his uneasiness Huck found himself drawing closer and closer to the alley, fearing all sorts of dreadful things, and momentarily expecting some catastrophe to happen that would take away his breath. There was not much to take away, for he seemed only able to inhale it by thimblefuls, and his heart would soon wear itself out, the way it was beating. Suddenly there was a flash of light, and Tom came tearing by him:

"Run!" said he. "Run for your life!"

He needn't have repeated it; once was enough; Huck was making thirty or forty miles an hour before the repetition was uttered. The boys never stopped till they reached the shed of a deserted slaughter-house at the lower end of the village. Just as they got within its shelter a storm burst and the rain poured down. As soon as Tom got his breath he said:

"Huck, it was awful! I tried two of the keys just as soft as I could; but they seemed to make such a power of racket that I couldn't hardly get my breath, I was so scared. They wouldn't turn in the lock either. Well, without noticing what I was doing, I took hold of the knob, and open comes the door! It wasn't locked! I hopped in and shook off the towel and, great Caesar's ghost!"

"What!—what'd you see, Tom?"

"Huck, I most stepped on to Injun Joe's hand!"

"No!"

"Yes. He was laying there, sound asleep on the floor, with his old patch on his eye and his arms spread out."

"Lordy, what did you do? Did he wake up?"

"No, never budged. Drunk, I reckon. I just grabbed that towel and started!"

"I'd never a thought of the towel, I bet!"

"Well, I would. My aunt would make me mighty sick if I lost it."

"Say, Tom, did you see that box?"

"Huck, I didn't wait to look around. I didn't see the box, I didn't see the cross. I didn't see anything but a bottle and a tin cup on the floor by Injun Joe! Yes, and I saw two barrels and lots more bottles in the room. Don't you see, now, what's the matter with that ha'nted room?"

"How?"

"Why, it's ha'nted with whisky! Maybe all the Temperance Taverns have got a ha'nted room?"

"Well, I reckon maybe that's so. Who'd a thought such a thing? But say, Tom, now's a mighty good time to get that box, if Injun Joe's drunk."

"It is that! You try it!"

"Well, no—I reckon not."

"And I reckon not, Huck. Only one bottle alongside of Injun Joe ain't enough. If there'd been three he'd be drunk enough and I'd do it." There was a long pause for reflection, and then Tom said:

"Looky here, Huck, let's not try that thing any more till we know Injun Joe's not there. It's too scary. Now if we watch every night, we'll be dead sure to see him go out some time or other, then we'll snatch that box quicker 'n lightning."

"Well, I'm agreed. I'll watch the whole night long, and I'll do it every night, too, if you'll do the other part of the job."

"All right, I will. All you got to do is to trot up Hooper Street a block and meow—and if I'm asleep, you throw some gravel at the window and that'll fetch me."

"Agreed, and good as wheat!"

"Now, Huck, the storm's over, and I'll go home. It'll begin to be daylight in a couple of hours. You go back and watch that long, will you?"

"I said I would, Tom, and I will. I'll ha'nt that tavern every night for a year. I'll sleep all day and I'll stand watch all night."

"That's all right. Now where are you going to sleep?"

"In Ben Roger's hayloft."

Becky's Picnic

The first thing Tom heard on Friday morning was a glad piece of news—Judge Thatcher's family had come back to town the night before, after spending the summer vacation in their Constantinople home. Both Injun Joe and the treasure sank into secondary importance for a moment, and Becky took the chief place in the boy's interest. He saw her, and they had an exhausting good time playing 'hi-spy' and 'gully-keeper' with a crowd of their schoolmates. The day was completed and crowned in a peculiarly satisfactory way: Becky teased her mother to appoint the next day for a picnic, and she consented. The child's delight was boundless, and Tom's not more moderate. The invitations were sent out before sunset, and straightway the young folks of the village were thrown into a fever of preparation and pleasureable anticipation. Tom's excitement enabled him to keep awake until a pretty late hour, and he had good hopes of hearing Huck's 'meow' and of having his treasure to astonish Becky and the picnickers with, next day; but he was disappointed. No signal came that night.

Morning came eventually, and by ten or eleven

o'clock a giddy and rollicking company were gathered at Judge Thatcher's, and everything was ready for a start. It was not the custom for elderly people to mar picnics with their presence. The children were considered safe enough under the wings of a few young ladies of eighteen and a few young gentlemen of twenty-three or thereabouts. The old steam ferry-boat was chartered for the occasion: presently the gay throng filed up the main street laden with provision baskets. Sid was sick and had to miss the fun; Mary remained at home to entertain him. The last thing Mrs Thatcher said to Becky was:

"You'll not get back till late. Perhaps you'd better stay all night with some of the girls that live near the ferry landing, child!"

"Then I'll stay with Susy Harper, mamma."

"Very well. And mind and behave yourself, and don't be any trouble."

Presently, as they tripped along, Tom said to Becky:

"Say—I'll tell you what we'll do. 'Stead of going to Joe Harper's, we'll climb right up the hill and stop at Widow Douglas's. She'll have ice-cream! She has it 'most every day—dead loads of it. And she'll be awful glad to have us."

"Oh, that will be fun!"

Then Becky reflected a moment, and said:

"But what will mamma say?"

"How'll she ever know?"

The girl turned the idea over in her mind, and said reluctantly:

"I reckon it's wrong—but——"

"But—shucks! Your mother won't know, and so what's the harm? All she wants is that you'll be safe; and I bet you she'd a said go there if she'd a thought of it. I know she would."

The Widow Douglas's splendid hospitality was a tempting bait. It and Tom's persuasions presently carried the day. So it was decided to say nothing to anybody about the night's programme.

Presently it occurred to Tom that maybe Huck might come this very night and give the signal. The thought took a deal of the spirit out of his anticipations. Still he could not bear to give up the fun at Widow Douglas's. And why should he give it up, he reasoned—the signal did not come the night before, so why should it be any more likely to come tonight? The sure fun of the evening outweighed the uncertain treasure; and, boy-like, he determined to

yield to the stronger inclination and not allow himself to think of the box of money another time that day.

Three miles below town, the ferry-boat stopped at the mouth of a woody hollow and tied up. The crowd swarmed ashore, and soon the forest distances and craggy heights echoed far and near with shouting and laughter. All the different ways of getting hot and tired were gone through with, and by-and-by the rovers straggled back to camp fortified with responsible appetites, and then the destruction of the good things began. After the feast there was a refreshing season of rest and chat in the shade of spreading oaks. By-and-by somebody shouted:

"Who's for the cave?"

Everybody was. Bundles of candles were produced, and straightway there was a general scamper up the hill. The mouth of the cave was high up the hill-side, an opening shaped like the letter A. Its massive oaken door stood unbarred. Within was a small chamber, chilly as an ice-house, and walled by Nature with solid lime-stone that was dewy with a cold sweat. It was romantic and mysterious to stand here in the deep gloom and look out upon the green valley shining in the sun.

The procession moved along the main avenue some three quarters of a mile, and then groups and couples began to slip aside into branch avenues, fly along the dismal corridors, and take each other by surprise at points where the corridors joined again.

Parties were able to elude each other for the space of half an hour without going beyond the 'known' ground.

By-and-by one group after another came straggling back to the mouth of the cave, panting, hilarious, smeared from head to foot with tallow drippings, daubed with clay, and entirely delighted with the success of the day. Then they were astonished to find that they had been taking no note of time, and that night was about at hand. The clanging bell had been calling for half an hour. However, this sort of close to the day's adventures was romantic and therefore satisfactory. When the ferry-boat with her wild freight pushed into the stream, nobody cared sixpence for the wasted time but the captain.

Huckleberry Finn to the Rescue

Huck was already upon his watch when the ferry-boat's lights went glinting past the wharf. Huck waited what seemed a weary long time when a noise fell upon his ear. He was all attention in an instant. The alley door closed softly. He sprang to the corner of the brick-store. The next moment two men brushed by him, and one seemed to have something under his arm. It must be that box! So they were going to remove the treasure. Why call Tom now? It would be absurd—the men would get away with the box and never be found again. No, he would stick to their wake and follow them; he would trust to the darkness for security from discovery. So Huck stepped out and glided along behind the men, like a cat, with bare feet, allowing them to keep just far enough ahead not to be visible.

He followed them a long way, through streets, past the quarry until they came to Widow Douglas's grounds. 'Very well', he thought, 'let them bury it there; it won't be hard to find.'

Now there was a low voice—Injun Joe's:

"Damn her, maybe she's got company—there's lights, late as it is."

"I can't see any."

This was that stranger's voice—the stranger of the haunted house. A deadly chill went to Huck's heart—this, then, was the 'revenge' job! His thought was to fly. Then he remembered that the Widow Douglas had been kind to him more than once, and maybe these men were going to murder her. He wished he dared venture to warn her; but he knew he didn't dare—they might come and catch him. He thought all this and more in the moment that elapsed between the stranger's remark and Injun Joe's next —which was:

"Because the bush is in your way. Now—this way —now you see, don't you?"

"Yes. Well, there is company there, I reckon. Better give it up."

"Give it up, and I just leaving this country for ever! Give it up, and maybe never have another chance. I tell you again, as I've told you before, I don't care for her swag—you may have it. But her husband was rough on me—many times he was rough on me—and mainly he was the justice of the peace that jugged me for a vagrant. And that ain't all! He had me horse-whipped! Like a nigger with all

the town looking on! Do you understand? He took advantage of me and died. But I'll take it out of her!"

"Oh, don't kill her! Don't do that!"

"Kill? Who said anything about killing? I would

66

kill him if he was here; but not her. When you want to get revenge on a woman you don't kill her—bosh! You go for her looks. You slit her nostrils—you notch her ears like a sow's!"

"By God, that's——"

"Keep your opinion to yourself! It will be safest for you. I'll tie her to the bed, and you'll help me —that's why you're here. If you flinch, I'll kill you! And if I have to kill you, I'll kill her—and then I reckon nobody'll ever know much about who done

67

this business. We'll wait till the lights are out, and we'll do it!"

Huck stepped gingerly back a few paces, then ran down past the quarry until he reached the old Welshman's cottage. He banged at the door, and presently the heads of the old man and his two stalwart sons were thrust from windows.

"What's the row there? Who's banging? What do you want?"

"Let me in—quick! I'll tell everything."

"Why, who are you?"

"Huckleberry Finn—quick, let me in!"

"Let him in, lads, and let's see what's the trouble."

"Please don't ever tell I told you," were Huck's first words when he got in. "Please don't—I'd be killed sure—but the Widow's been good friend to me sometimes, and I want to tell—I will tell if you'll promise you won't ever say it was me."

"By George, he has got something to tell, or he

wouldn't act so!" exclaimed the old man. "Out with it, and nobody here'll ever tell, lad."

Three minutes later the old man and his sons, well armed, were up the hill, and just entering the path on tip-toe, their weapons in their hands. Huck accompanied them no farther. He hid behind a great boulder and fell to listening. There was a lagging, anxious silence, and then all of a sudden there was an explosion of firearms and a cry. Huck waited for no particulars. He sprang away and sped down the hill as fast as his legs could carry him.

Huckleberry Finn the Hero

As the earliest suspicion of dawn appeared on Sunday morning, Huck came groping up the hill and rapped gently at the old Welshman's door. The inmates were asleep, but it was a sleep that was set on a hair-trigger, on account of the exciting episode of the night. A call came from a window:

"Who's there?"

Huck's scared voice answered in a low tone:

"Do please let me in! It's only Huck Finn!"

"It's a name that can open this door night or day, lad! Welcome!"

These were strange words to the vagabond boy's ears, and the pleasantest he had ever heard. He could not recollect that the closing word had ever been applied in his case before.

The door was quickly unlocked and he entered. Huck was given a seat, and the old man and his brace of tall sons speedily dressed themselves.

"Now, my boy, I hope you're good and hungry, because breakfast will be ready as soon as the sun's up, and we'll have a piping hot one, too—make yourself easy about that. I and the boys hoped you'd turn up and stop here last night."

"I was awful scared," said Huck, "and I run. I took out when the pistols went off, and I didn't stop for three mile. I've come now becuz I wanted to know about it, you know; and I come before daylight becuz I didn't want to run into them devils, even if they was dead."

"Well, poor chap, you do look as if you'd had a hard time of it—but there's a bed here for you when you've had your breakfast," said the Welshman.

Just as breakfast was completed there was a knock at the door. Huck jumped for a hiding-place, for he had no mind to be connected even remotely with the late event. The Welshman admitted several ladies and gentlemen, among them the Widow Douglas, and noticed that groups of citizens were climbing the hill to stare at the stile. So the news had spread.

The Welshman had to tell the story of the night to the visitors. The Widow's gratitude for her preservation was outspoken.

"Don't say a word about it, madam. There's another that you're more beholden to than you are to me and my boys maybe, but he don't allow me to tell his name. We wouldn't ever have been there but for him."

Of course this excited a curiosity so vast that it almost belittled the main matter.

Tom and Becky Missing

Mrs Thatcher addressed Mrs Harper:

"Is my Becky going to sleep all day?"

"Your Becky?"

"Yes," with a startled look. "Didn't she stay with you last night?"

"Why, no."

Mrs Thatcher turned pale, and sank into a chair just as Aunt Polly, talking briskly with a friend, approached, and said:

"Good morning Mrs Thatcher, good morning, Mrs Harper, my Tom seems to be missing, did he stay with either of you last night?"

"He didn't stay with us," said Mrs Harper, beginning to look uneasy. A marked anxiety came into Aunt Polly's face.

Early in the forenoon of the next day parties of jaded men began to straggle into the village after a long search, but the strongest of the citizens continued searching for the pair. All the news that could be gained was that remotenesses of the cavern were being ransacked that had never been visited before; that every corner and crevice was going to be thoroughly searched; that wherever one wandered through the maze of passages, lights were to be seen flitting hither and thither in the distance, and shoutings and pistol-shots sent their hollow reverberations to the ear down the sombre aisles. In one place, far from the section usually traversed by tourists, the names 'Becky' and 'Tom' had been found traced upon the rocky wall with candle smoke, and near at hand a grease-soiled bit of ribbon.

Lost in the Cave

Now to return to Tom and Becky's share in the picnic. Tom had found a subterranean lake which stretched its dim length away until its shape was lost in the shadows. He wanted to explore its borders, but concluded that it would be best to sit down and rest a while first. Now for the first time the deep stillness of the place laid a clammy hand upon the spirits of the children. Becky said:

"Why, I didn't notice, but it seems ever so long since I heard any of the others."

"Come to think, Becky, we are away down below them, and we couldn't hear them here."

Becky grew apprehensive.

"I wonder how long we've been down here, Tom? We better start back."

"Yes, I reckon we better."

"Can you find the way, Tom? It's all a mixed-up crookedness to me."

"I reckon I could find it, but then the bats. If they put both our candles out, it will be an awful fix. Let's try some other way, so as not to go through there."

"Well, but I hope we won't get lost. It would be so awful!" and the child shuddered at the thought of the dreadful possibilities.

They started through a corridor, and traversed it in silence a long way, glancing at each new opening, to see if there was anything familiar about the look of it; but they were all strange. Every time Tom made an examination, Becky would watch his face for an encouraging sign, and he would say cheerily:

"Oh, it's all right. This ain't the one, but we'll come to it right away!" But he felt less and less hopeful with each failure, and presently began to turn off into diverging avenues at sheer random, in the desperate hope of finding the one that was wanted. He still said it was 'All right' but there was such a leaden dread at his heart, that the words had lost their ring, and sounded as if he had said, 'All is lost!' Becky clung to his side in an anguish of fear, and tried hard to keep back the tears, but they would come. At last she said:

"Oh, Tom, let's go back that way! We seem to get worse off all the time."

Tom stopped.

"Listen!" said he.

Profound silence; silence so deep that even their breathings were conspicuous in the hush. Tom shouted. The call went echoing down the empty aisles, and died out in the distance in a faint sound that resembled a ripple of mocking laughter.

"Oh, don't do it again, Tom, it is too horrid," said Becky.

"It is horrid, but I better, Becky; they might hear us, you know," and he shouted again.

They moved on and by-and-by Tom took Becky's candle and blew it out. This economy meant so much. Words were not needed. Becky understood, and her hope died again. She knew that Tom had a whole candle and three or four pieces in his pocket——yet he must economise.

The children wandered about more passages uselessly then groped their way to a spring to rest and eat some remains of cake they had left from the picnic. The weary time dragged on; they slept and awoke famished and woe-stricken. They had lost all sense of time.

Now an idea struck Tom. There were some side-passages near at hand. It would be better to explore some of these than bear the weight of the heavy time in idleness. He took a kite-line from his pocket, tied it to a projection, and he and Becky started, Tom in the lead, unwinding the line as he groped along. At the end of twenty steps the corridor ended in a 'jumping-off' place. Tom got down on his knees and felt below, and then as far around the corner as he could reach with his hands conveniently; he made an effort to stretch yet a little further to the right, and at the moment, a short distance away, a human hand, holding a candle, appeared from behind a rock! Tom lifted up a glorious shout, and instantly that hand was followed by the body it belonged to—Injun Joe's! Tom was paralysed; he could not move. He was vastly gratified the next moment to see the Spaniard take to his heels and get himself out of sight. Tom wondered that Joe had not recognised his voice, and come over and killed him for testifying in court. But the echoes must have disguised the voice. Without that was it, he reasoned. Tom's fright weakened every muscle in his body. He said to himself that if he had strength enough to get back to the spring he would stay there, and nothing should tempt him to run the risk of meeting Injun Joe again. He was careful to keep from Becky what it was that he had seen. He told her he had only shouted 'for luck'.

But hunger and wretchedness rise superior to fears in the long run. Another tedious wait at the spring, and another long sleep brought changes. The

children awoke, tortured with a raging hunger. Tom believed it must be Wednesday or Thursday or even Friday or Saturday now, and if there was a search for them, it had been given over. He proposed to explore another passage. He felt willing to risk Injun Joe and all other terrors. But Becky was very weak. She had sunk into a dreary apathy, and would not be roused. She told Tom to go with the kite-line and explore if he chose; but she implored him to come back every little while and speak to her.

Tom kissed her, with a choking sensation in his throat, and made a show of being confident of finding the searchers or an escape from the cave; then he took the kite-line in his hand and went groping down one of the passages on his hands and knees, distressed with hunger and sick with bodings of coming doom. . . .

Home Again

Tom lay upon a sofa with an eager auditory about him, and told the history of the wonderful adventure, putting in many striking additions to adorn it withal; and closed with a description of how he left Becky and went on an exploring expedition; how he followed two avenues as far as his kite-line would reach; how he followed a third to the fullest stretch of the kite-line, and was about to turn back when he glimpsed a far-off speck that looked like daylight; dropped the line and groped towards it, pushed his head and shoulders through a small hole and saw the broad Mississippi rolling by! And if it had only happened to be night he would not have seen that speck of daylight, and would not have explored that passage any more! He told how he went back for Becky and broke the good news, and she told him not to fret her with such stuff, for she was tired, and knew she was going to die, and wanted to. He described how he laboured with her and convinced her, and how she almost died for joy when she had groped to where she actually saw the blue speck of daylight; how he pushed his way out of the hole and then helped her out; how they sat there and cried for gladness; how some men came along in a skiff, and Tom hailed them and told them their situation and their famished condition; how the men didn't believe the wild tale at first, "because," said they, "you are five miles down the river below the valley the cave is in"; then took them aboard, rowed to a house, gave them supper, made them rest till two or three hours after dark, and then brought them home.

After a couple of weeks passed and Tom had recovered, he decided to stop by and see Becky, who was growing stronger now. The Judge was there and said:

"Well, at least nobody will get lost in that cave any more."

"Why?"

"Because I had its big door sheathed with boiler iron two weeks ago, and triple locked; and I've got the keys."

Tom turned as white as a sheet.

"What's the matter, boy? Here, run, somebody! Fetch a glass of water!"

The water was brought and thrown into Tom's face.

"Ah, now you're all right. What was the matter with you, Tom?"

"Oh, Judge, Injun Joe's in the cave!"

Final Search for Injun Joe

Within a few minutes the news had spread, and a dozen skiff-loads of men were on their way to McDougal's cave, and the ferry-boat, well filled with passengers, soon followed. Tom Sawyer was in the skiff that bore Judge Thatcher. When the cave door was unlocked, a sorrowful sight presented itself in the dim twilight of the place. Injun Joe lay stretched upon the ground, dead, with his face close to the crack of the door, as if his longing eyes had been fixed to the latest moment upon the light and the cheer of the free world outside.

Injun Joe was buried near the mouth of the cave; and people flocked there in boats and wagons from the town and from all the farms and hamlets for seven miles around. They brought their children and all sorts of provisions, and confessed that they had had almost as satisfactory a time at the funeral as they could have had at the hanging.

The morning after the funeral, Tom took Huck to a private place to have an important talk. Huck had just found out that the Temperance Tavern had been closed down for selling whisky. He knew all about Tom's adventure from the Welshman and the Widow Douglas by this time, but Tom said he reckoned there was one thing they had not told him. Huck's face saddened. He said:

"I know what it is. You got into number two, and never found anything but whisky. Nobody told me it was you, but I just knowed it must a ben you, soon as I heard 'bout that whisky business; and I knowed you hadn't got the money becuz you'd a got at me some way or other, and told me, even if you was mum to everybody else. Tom, something's always told me we'd never get hold of that swag.

"Why, Huck, I never told on that tavern-keeper. You know his tavern was all right the Saturday I went to the picnic. Don't you remember you was to watch there that night?"

"Oh, yes! Why it seems 'bout a year ago. It was that very night that I follered Injun Joe."

"You followed him?"

"Yes—but you keep mum. I reckon Injun Joe's left friends behind him. I don't want 'em souring on me, and doing me mean tricks. If it hadn't been for me he'd be down in Texas now, all right."

Then Huck told his entire adventure in confidence to Tom, who had only heard of the Welshman's part of it before.

"Well," said Huck presently, coming back to the

main question, "whoever nipped the whisky in number two nipped the money too, I reckon—anyways it's a goner for us, Tom."

"Huck, that money wasn't ever in number two!"

"What!" Huck searched his comrade's face keenly. "Tom, have you got on the track of that money again?"

"Huck, it's in the cave!"

Huck's eyes blazed.

"Say it again, Tom!"

"The money's in the cave!"

"Tom—honest injun, now—is it fun or earnest?"

"Earnest, Huck—just as earnest as ever I was in my life. Will you go with me and help get it out?"

"I bet I will! I will if it's where we can blaze our way to it and not get lost."

"Huck, we can do that without the least little bit of trouble in the world. I'll take you right to it in a skiff, the way that nobody but me knows of!"

"Let's start right off, Tom!"

Finding the Treasure

They got to the hole where Tom had discovered the speck of daylight and climbed inside, Tom in the lead. The boys began to quiet down to whispers, now, for the stillness and gloom of the place oppressed their spirits. They went on with their kite-lines and presently entered and followed a corridor until they reached the 'jumping-off place'. Their candles revealed the fact that it was not really a precipice, but only a steep clay hill. Tom whispered:

"Now I'll show you something, Huck."

He held his candle aloft and said:

"Look as far around the corner as you can. Do you see that? There—on the big rock over yonder—done with candle smoke."

"Tom, it's a cross!"

"Now where's your number two? 'Under the cross', hey? Right yonder's where I saw Injun Joe poke up his candle, Huck. We'll climb down there and have a hunt for that box."

Tom went first, cutting rude steps in the clay hill as he descended. Huck followed. Four avenues opened out of the small cavern which the great rock stood in. The boys examined three of them with no result. They found a small recess in the one nearest the base of the rock, with a pallet of blankets spread down in it; but there was no money-box. The lads

searched and re-searched this place but in vain.

Then, Tom said:

"Looky here, Huck, there's foot-prints and some candle-grease on the clay about one side of this rock, but not on the other sides. Now, what's that for? I bet you the money is under the rock. I'm going to dig in the clay."

Then Huck began to dig and scratch also. Some boards were soon uncovered and removed. They had concealed a natural chasm which led under the rock. Tom got into this and held his candle as far under the rock as he could, but said he could not see the end of the rift. He proposed to explore. He stooped and passed under; the narrow way descended gradually. He followed its winding course, first to the right, then to the left, Huck at his heels. Tom turned a short curve by-and-by, and exclaimed:

"My goodness, Huck, looky here!"

It was the treasure-box sure enough, occupying a snug little cavern.

"Got it at last!" said Huck, ploughing among the tarnished coins with his hands. "My, but we're rich, Tom!"

"Huck, I always reckoned we'd get it. It's just too good to believe, but we have got it, sure! Say, let's not fool around here, let's snake it out. Lemme see if I can lift the box."

It weighed about fifty pounds. Tom could lift it after an awkward fashion, but could not carry it conveniently.

"I thought so," he said: "they carried it like it was heavy that day at the ha'nted house—I noticed that. I reckon I was right to think of fetching the money bags along."

The money was soon in the bags, and the boys took it up to the cross rock.

They presently emerged into a clump of bushes, looked warily out, found the coast clear, and were soon lunching in the skiff. As the sun dipped towards the horizon they pushed out and got under way. Tom skimmed up the shore through the long twilight, chattering cheerily to Huck, and landed shortly after dark.

"Now, Huck," said Tom, "we'll hide the money in the loft of the Widow's wood shed, and I'll come up in the morning and we'll count and divide, and then we'll hunt up a place out in the woods for it where it will be safe. Just you lay quiet here and watch the stuff till I run and hook Benny Taylor's little wagon. I won't be a minute."

He disappeared, and presently returned with the wagon, put the bags into it, threw some old rags on top of them, and started off, dragging his cargo behind him. When the boys reached the Welshman's house they stopped to rest. Just as they were about to move on, the Welshman stepped out and said:

"Hallo, who's that?"

"Huck and Tom Sawyer."

"Good! Come along with me, boys, you are keeping everybody waiting. Here, hurry up, trot ahead; I'll haul the wagon for you. Why, it's not as light as it might be. Got bricks in it, or old metal?"

"Old metal," said Tom.

"I judged so; the boys in this town will take more trouble and fool away more time hunting up six bits' worth of old iron to sell to the foundry, than they would to make twice the money at regular work. But that's human nature. Hurry along, hurry along!"

The boys wanted to know what the hurry was about.

"Never mind; you'll see when we get to the Widow Douglas's."

Huck said with some apprehension, for he was long used to being falsely accused:

"We haven't been doing nothing."

"Well, I don't know, Huck, my boy. I don't know about that. Ain't you and the Widow good friends?"

"Yes. Well, she's ben a good friend to me, anyways."

"All right, then. What do you want to be afraid for?"

This question was not entirely answered in Huck's slow mind before he found himself pushed, along with Tom, into Mrs Douglas's drawing-room. The Welshman left the wagon near the door and followed.

The Final Reward

The place was grandly lighted, and everybody that was of any consequence in the village was there. The Thatchers were there, the Harpers, the Rogerses, Aunt Polly, Sid, Mary, the minister, the editor, and a great many more, and all dressed in their best. The Widow received the boys as heartily as anyone could well receive two such looking beings. They were covered with clay and candle-grease. Aunt Polly blushed crimson with humiliation, and frowned and shook her head at Tom. Nobody suffered half as much as the two boys did, however. The Welshman said:

"Tom wasn't at home, yet, so I gave him up; but I stumbled on him and Huck right at my door, and so I just brought them along in a hurry."

"And you did just right," said the Widow. "Come with me, boys."

She took them to a bedchamber and said:

"Now wash and dress yourselves. Here are two new suits of clothes—shirts, socks, everything complete. They're Huck's—no, no thanks, Huck—the Welshman, Mr Jones, bought one and I the other. But they'll fit both of you. Get into them. We'll wait—come down when you are slicked up enough."

Then she left.

After they had put on their new togs, which made Huck so disgusted, Tom knew he'd be back in his old rags as soon as he could, they went downstairs.

The Widow was so grateful for Huck's part in saving her from Injun Joe, she promised him a home with her and money for a business.

"But Huck don't need it," Tom said. "He's rich. Huck's got money. Maybe you don't believe it, but he's got lots of it. Oh, you needn't smile, I reckon I can show you. You just wait a minute." And they both ran out to the wagon and brought in the money bags. Everyone gasped when they counted out twelve thousand dollars, which was more than anyone present had ever seen at one time before, and after explanations it was agreed that the money should be invested for them.

The weeks passed but Huck was none too happy under the Widow's discipline and being rich didn't impress him either, so one day he ran off. Tom found him three days later, and after promising him that he could join his 'robber gang', got him to go back to the Widow's home, and that's where he's been ever since that day.